CU00796320

HANDOL AND DOUDOL AND OTHER STORIES

Errezzaki El Hassan

MINERVA PRESS

LONDON
MONTREUX LOS ANGELES SYDNEY

HANDOL AND DOUDOL AND OTHER STORIES
Copyright © Errezzaki El Hassan 1998

All Rights Reserved

ISBN 1 86106 671 6

First Published 1998 by
MINERVA PRESS
195 Knightsbridge
London SW7 1RE

Printed in Great Britain for Minerva Press

HANDOL AND DOUDOL
AND OTHER STORIES

Contents

A Korean Story

Handol and Doudol

Once upon a time, two children lived in a tiny village at Mount Keumgang in Korea. The first was called Handol, while the latter was known as Doudol.

The two poor children had no one but their two old mothers. Their fathers, who had taken part in the war many years before, had died in the same battle.

The loss of their fathers made them twin brothers rather than intimate friends; when one of them found by chance a single fruit floating on the surface of the water, while they jumped near the river, or when a handful of hazelnuts was given to them, they shared everything with a good heart.

On a spring day when they were eighteen years old, many policemen came and declared that they had to join the army. They forced them to obey immediately.

"The skin of the father, is it not sufficient? Why do you need more? My only son?"

"What a shame to break my heart!"

The two widows protested but the policemen turned a deaf ear.

Thus Doudol and Handol became soldiers, but they couldn't sleep peacefully and they lost their appetites when they thought about their poor mothers.

One day, Handol suffered a great misfortune. When he was on guard at night near the provisions warehouse, many hundreds of rice sacks were stolen. After a quick trial, he was condemned to death and thrown into prison.

Doudol soon heard the terrible news that Handol's mother had a grave sickness. But, perceiving that the adjutant didn't want to inform Handol, he decided to visit his friend in his cell in order to explain the family situation, and to advise him to apply for a permit to see his sick mother.

The officer refused rudely, "In the course of five days, he will be executed. Why should I let him see his mother?"

Doudol was heartbroken. The imminent loss of his friend, unjustly accused, was unbearable.

He wondered what he could do to allow Handol to see his mother. He was very anxious and he presented himself again at the chief's office.

"Put me in prison in place of Handol and let him go home," suggested Doudol politely. The officer was amazed, as the condemned was going to be executed in the course of a few days.

The officer heard of the intense ties between the two boys, but the proposition was more surprising than touching. After a moment he declared: "You must die instead of your friend if he doesn't come back on time. Do you understand?"

"I am sure he will come back on time, unless an accident happens and obliges him not to come back on time. Then you would have the right to execute me," Doudol said courageously.

The officer didn't object.

Before he went home, Handol embraced Doudol and cried loudly, shedding tears. The scene was very touching. The jailers themselves couldn't restrain their emotions.

Leaving the prison, Handol came back to his native village after two days. He first visited Doudol's mother, but nobody was to be found. He turned home where he found Doudol's mother taking care of his own sick mother.

"Mother!" he cried with a down-hearted tone.

"It's you, Handol! Thank God!"

Delighted, Doudol's mother rushed to meet him. But his sick mother, lying as if she was dead, didn't recognise her beloved son.

"How is my beloved son, Doudol?" Doudol's mother asked, patting Handol on the shoulders.

"Oh, yes! All... all right," stuttered Handol, feeling guilty about telling the lie.

"You've come just in time. Your mother seems incapable of recovering tonight. But she may get up when she sees you."

Doudol's mother led him to his mother's bed and he whispered in his mother's ear, "Mummy it's me. I'm Handol." But she didn't react; her eyes remained closed. "Mummy, Mummy..." Handol called out anxiously trying to awake her, but to no avail.

The next morning, the sick woman had not yet regained consciousness. She was in agony and therefore it was impossible for him to leave his mother's bed. But he thought constantly about his detained friend.

He whispered, "Doudol, I know there is no such true friend as you. I'm coming, please don't worry." He clenched his teeth. "My mother's disease is now incurable. And I feel some consolation at least, as I am seeing my mother before her death. I can't let Doudol die in my place, at any rate."

Handol stood up and said to Doudol's mother, "Mummy, will you please look after my mother? I must go now."

"What did you say? How dare you leave your agonised mother?" The woman was astonished.

"Excuse me. I must go!" said Handol, shedding tears as he couldn't reveal the secret.

"What? The discipline is so cruel? No, you mustn't go."

The woman seized his hand, but Handol insisted. "Mummy, let me go. I'll explain the whole matter later on. Now, I can't say anything more."

"What has happened to you that you can't speak now? If you insist, I won't tell you anything. Don't worry any more about your mother. Have a safe journey."

As she had promised, she didn't add anything as if she was a mute. Handol bowed profoundly in front of his unconscious mother and left the house in tears.

The fifth day arrived. Talk, blaming Handol, began to spread in the barracks.

"I wonder what he is thinking of. They seem intimate, but Handol hasn't come yet after exposing his friend to such danger."

"Doudol is unfortunate indeed, he is losing his life because of his friend."

The thought of the unjust death of Doudol prompted all his companions to take pity on him, as the time for his execution came finally.

With a raising head, Doudol walked calmly towards the precipice. His companions cried, "Doudol, my friend!" He turned to them and made an amicable sign.

When he arrived at the precipice edge the officer asked him, "Haven't you regretted?"

"Never. I've no regret. I am rather happy as I pave the way for my friend to see his mother. I'm sure he is coming back this moment and my last hope is to keep him alive if he comes back," said Doudol calmly.

"Good. I'll do what you say."

The officer moved back and raised a hand. The soldiers of the platoon raised their bows and strained the strings.

The officer prepared to signal the execution, when the clip-clop of horse's hooves were heard in the valley. He turned his head towards the place where the sounds had come from. A running white horse arrived, raising a storm of dust. The horseman, waving his hands, shouted loudly, "This horseman is Handol, isn't he?" a soldier asked.

"Perhaps," another replied.

The agitation spread among the crowd which looked at the scene curiously. In the twinkling of an eye, the horse arrived at the precipice and Handol jumped down screaming, "Doudol!" He threw himself down and embraced his friend with open arms.

"Here I am. Execute me!" he said, panting, to the soldiers of the platoon.

Breathless, he fixed his eyes on the archers. The crowd was astonished. Doudol had never thought that his friend would have come back in five days, thinking that he would still be looking after his sick mother.

"Handol!"

"Doudol!"

After calling each other, they embraced.

"Handol, did you see your mother?"

"Yes, I saw yours too."

"Why do you return instead of treating your mother?"

"What did you say? Was it reasonable to let you die in my place? What would I do without you?"

Handol hugged his friend, saying, "Doudol, you looked so grief-stricken because of me. I should have been here earlier, but..." looking at him with extreme concern, Handol recounted the following: after he had visited his sick mother, Handol had hurried to return. When crossing a col between two high mountains, he had tripped over a stone and fallen to the ground. He had sprained an ankle and lost the ability to walk. Handol had lamented because of his damaged foot.

"Doudol, Doudol! You will die in my place!"

A hair merchant who was crossing the col at that moment heard the lamentations and turned to him. He listened to the young man's story and said to him, "Your true friendship is very touching. Now, ride the horse immediately!" The merchant offered him the bridle of a white horse. Handol rode non-stop to the barracks.

All the soldiers were astonished by this strange story. The effort of one friend to save his friend from death was as touching as the voluntary sacrifice of the other.

The officer, who observed the movements of his men, reflected a moment and addressed Handol,

"Handol. Now, it's you who will die. Be ready!" he shouted, fixing mocking eyes on him.

"After all this, he will die?"

"Monster! It's a veritable monster!"

The crowd was then in turmoil.

At this moment, a voice screamed, "My friends! I am telling the truth." An old soldier advanced. "It's our officer who stole the provisions!"

"How did this happen?"

All were surprised by this unexpected accusation.

"Rascal! How dare you tell us this?" The officer intended to kill the old soldier.

"That night," the accuser continued, "I was on patrol. I saw him with my own eyes, plundering the warehouse with a gang of thieves. I was a veritable imbecile as I feared the perpetrator of the theft, and I dared not inform against him. It's me that should be punished. Come on! Kill me in the place of Handol." He lamented, beating his chest and shedding tears.

A voice shouted, "Kill the officer!"

"Kill the thief!" shouted another.

The furious soldiers, spears raised, circled the criminal and the officer was executed.

Thereafter, the sick mother recovered and Handol and Doudol returned to their native village where they lived long and happy lives.

A Chinese Story

The Two Brothers

Yu Po-Ya was an official of high rank in the kingdom of China during the epoch of Spring and Autumn (722–484 BC). One day, he decided to go on a trip, so he went boating. But suddenly, an unexpected storm broke up his enjoyment of the calm river. Rapidly, he anchored the boat by attaching it to a solid rock.

After the rain had been pouring hard all day, the plain moon came into sight; this was the day of the moon festival. Yu started playing a 'Qin', his favourite stringed instrument. All of a sudden, the Qin went out of tune because one string broke. He was astonished as nobody was in sight and his anxiety multiplied; he said to himself, 'If there is no habitation here, nobody will hear me. But a string has broken. That means someone has been listening, and he may be a thief or a killer who lies in wait for me.'

Yu ordered his guards: "Hurry up! Disembark! Go on to the bank, and keep yourselves out of sight!"

While the men were preparing to disembark, they heard a soft voice coming from the bank saying, "Don't worry. I am a woodcutter and not a thief or a killer. I was passing here when your nice music attracted me, so I stopped to listen."

Yu examined the stranger with furtive eyes and said, laughing, "A woodcutter who has been listening to my music? I wonder if you know a single note? Anyway, this has no importance. Now, go away!"

But the woodcutter refused to move, saying, "You are totally wrong. Who has said a woodcutter knows no music?

Haven't you heard that there is a man of value in every ten houses, and that this man always meets a visitor of his own rank? So, if you think I know no music, then you won't sing any more."

Impressed greatly by his saying, Yu asked, "If you are listening sincerely to my music, then what was I playing?"

"You were playing a piece describing the lamentation of Confucius the sage after the death of Yen Hui, and you didn't finish but the first three lines. One string broke in the fourth sentence!"

"You know truly the music," said Yu with admiration. He invited the woodcutter immediately to get into the boat. This latter was obliged to acquiesce. He wore a straw hat to protect him from the rain, a coat of coco fibres and straw sandals. He carried an axe and a bamboo basket. A servant told him,

"You! Pay attention to your language when speaking with our master. He is an official of high rank."

After taking off his hat, the woodcutter entered the cabin and said, bowing, "Enchanted, sir."

Seeing him bowing instead of kneeling, Yu was a little vexed. He said, raising his hand to reply to the woodcutter's greetings, "Enchanted."

He ordered the servants to fetch a chair. A chair was brought and the woodcutter took a seat without uttering a word. The functionary decided to ask his visitor his name, and to bring him some tea. After a long moment, the host broke the silence.

"Thus, it was you who had been listening to my music."

"Yes."

"Therefore, you must have known certain things about the Qin."

At this moment, the captain came to announce that it was time to sail. Yu told him to wait one moment.

The woodcutter said then, "I ought not to detain you."

Yu replied, with a mocking tone, "Don't you want to tell that you only know a little about the Qin?" The woodcutter started a long speech about the structure of the Qin. Suspecting his answer to be a result of a strong memory, Yu decided to test him.

"If you know about music to such extent, then you'll know that Yen Hui was capable of reading the music of Confucius the sage." He continued, "One day, when the sage had been playing the Qin, Yen Hui entered. Sensing death in his master's music, Yen found this very strange and asked the master why. Confucius replied, 'While I was playing, I saw a cat pursuing a mouse. I desired truly that it should have captured it but I feared too that it had missed it. All that had been in my mind was reflected on my music, and it was death which you felt.'"

"Now," said Yu, "If I play, do you think you'll be able to know what's in my mind?"

The woodcutter replied, "I'll try, but don't get angry if I fail."

Yu put a new string in and repaired his Qin, meditating for a moment. Then he started to play, imagining the high mountains in his mind.

When Yu finished his music, the woodcutter clapped his hands and said, "It was splendid! You represented the high mountains in your mind."

Yu kept silent and remained sitting to meditate. Then, he returned to music, imagining the flowing water. When he had finished, the woodcutter said, "It was marvellous! You were thinking of the flowing water."

Amazed, Yu stood and bowed to the woodcutter.

He said to him, "I beg your pardon for I have been impolite. I'll never judge people by their appearances. May I ask you your name, sir?"

The woodcutter replied, "My family name is Chung, my name is Hui, and I have also another name: Tzu-Chi." After he had introduced himself briefly, Yu ordered tea for his visitor and asked, "Excuse me for being somehow impolite, but why are you content as a woodcutter? With your talents you could have fame and fortune. It's a shame."

Chung said, "My parents are old and I am their only son. I prefer to remain with them for the rest of their life."

Yu was obliged to admire Chung for such filial piety and they became absorbed in discussion, Yu respected and admired Chung more and more. Finally, Yu suggested that they should become sworn brothers.

Chung said, "You are surely joking! You are a high-ranking officer, while I am a mere woodcutter from a poor village. You'll suffer dishonour by such an engagement."

Yu said, "But, where can I find a friend like you who is able to read my mind? It's a great honour to have known you. Who do you think I am, a man who considers only the social rank?" Yu immediately ordered candles and incense to be lit. They became sworn brothers after a simple ritual, and chattered all night long without showing any sign of fatigue. Finally, the day dawned bright and fair, and it was high time for Yu to sail.

While Chung was getting up to leave, Yu held his hand and said, "Alas, my brother we have been acquainted too late and we have to separate so soon. How about going with me for some days?"

Chung replied, "This pleases me very much, but my parents are old and I can't leave them."

Yu said, "In this case, I will come back to see you next year." They agreed to meet after a year at the same time and in the same place. Then, Yu offered Chung some gold and some presents for his parents. Finally they separated.

The days passed quickly, and the time for the meeting approached. Yu could not wait and went searching for his friend. His boat arrived finally at its destination. He anchored at the same rock where he had met Chung for the first time.

The full moon of the mid-autumn festival was bright as usual, but Chung didn't appear. Yu said to himself, "Perhaps he doesn't recognise my boat, which I have changed. I'll play some music, and then he must come." So Yu asked for his Qin and started playing. But he stopped immediately as he had discovered that one string was repeating a sad sound. Yu said,

"Something must have happened to my brother. Maybe one of his parents is dead, and this is why he hasn't appeared. I will pay him a visit."

The next morning, Yu set off early, followed by a servant who carried his Qin. But the two were bewildered when they arrived at a cross-roads. At that moment, they saw an old man coming towards them. After he had ascertained their direction, the old man asked them who they wanted to visit as he knew everybody in the neighbourhood.

Yu said, "I intend to visit a friend called Tzu-Chi." Hearing this name, the old man burst into tears before wailing sharply with terror.

He said, "He is my beloved son! A year ago he met a high-ranking officer called Yu Po-Ya, and they became good friends. Mr Yu gave him some gold with which my son bought a lot of books. He worked hard during the day and studied conscientiously all night. Some months ago, he was taken ill and he died a hundred days ago."

Hearing this bad news, Yu collapsed onto the ground, crying, and began to swoon.

Very surprised, the old man threw himself down beside Yu and asked the servant who the man was. The servant replied, "He is Mr Yu Po-Ya."

When Yu had recovered, he sat down on the floor, beating his chest and crying with a great sorrow. He asked the old man, "Where was Tzu-Chi buried?"

The old man replied, "Just beyond a cliff not far from here. He said that he had an appointment with you there. I have just come from the place where his grave lies."

Yu asked the old man to go along with him to his friend's grave. Arriving there, he cried so loudly that all villagers rushed to them. Yu had nothing to sacrifice but his Qin. He started to play, surrounded by the curious villagers. But when he finished, the crowd laughed foolishly and dispersed quickly. Yu turned to the old man and asked, "What are they laughing at? I am so upset."

The old man said, "They don't appreciate your music."

Yu asked him then, "And you, do you know what I played?"

The old man replied, "I am afraid I don't know anything."

Yu started then to explain the air and words which he had composed. When he had finished the last two lines he said, "When this song ends, the Qin will die for you."

He took out a knife from his pocket, and cut all the strings of the instrument. Thereupon, he raised the instrument and threw it onto the tombstone. The Qin was torn to pieces and the terrified old man asked, "Why have you done this?"

Yu said, "Now that Tzu-Chi is dead, nobody can understand my music. I'll never play again."

Yu asked the old man to accept all the gold that he had brought and he promised to return to search for him and his wife, in order to accompany them to his house, Yu said, "From now on, I am Tzu-Chi and I'll be beside you for the rest of your life."

Yu didn't go until he had lamented for his beloved friend and brother for many hours.

A Danish Story

The Treasure

The surprise made an intense impression on him, as becoming wealthy and possessing gold and silver was something which he had never expected in his life. One day, while he was ploughing his field, his axe struck strongly against an iron box. At first blush, he mistook it for a stone. When he discovered that it was a real box, he hastened to dust it off. At night when it was dark, he returned to the field and carried the box home. Then, he went to bed free from worry, as he realised that the treasure was his own property.

The man decided not to reveal anything about his treasure for fear that the tyrannous greedy governor might seize it, as he always used to demand that the peasants gave him half of their harvests.

But the man didn't make any effort to conceal the news from his stupid wife. The woman tried to hide the matter from everyone but she told a few friends of hers, advising them not to tell anyone. The news became widespread and widely known all over the village.

One day, the wife heard a sharp knock on the door, and she was surprised when the governor threatened and menaced her with a severe punishment if she refused to reveal the secret of the treasure that her husband had found. The poor wife couldn't resist the threat and she told him everything.

The governor returned to his palace after he had heard everything, while the woman remained in her place trembling with fear, awaiting the return of her husband. When she told him what had happened, his body shook with rage. But he controlled himself quickly turning to the door and going out.

The man saddled his horse in the garden and bound it to the cart. He called his wife to go for a ride, and they went at high speed to the city.

The cart stopped in front of a luxurious restaurant in the city. The man invited his wife to a delicious meal which she ate with a good appetite. Meanwhile, he hid his treasure in a safe place. Coming back, he carried a big box full of dried figs.

On returning in the evening, the wind was blowing and the rain had been falling.

Fatigue and indigestion affected the woman till she fell into a deep sleep. Suddenly, she was awakened by a strong blow on her head. She was surprised when she discovered that the blow was caused only by some dried figs. She stood, glaring and breathing heavily, and said to her husband, "What's happened here? What are these figs?"

"There was a terrible storm, so heavy that the figs fell with the rain!"

The woman returned to her deep sleep and the cart went on at full speed. Eventually, it came near the governor's palace. She was awakened by an abominable sound of braying, and she screamed, "What am I hearing? Where do these abominable sounds come from?"

The man whispered in her ear, "Speak in a low voice! The sound is the screaming of the governor. The gang boss is lashing him with a whip, because he has called him to pay the accounts and the governor has refused to pay the debt."

Then, the woman cried, "Let's go away immediately! I am afraid of the gangsters."

After a moment, when the woman had calmed down, her husband said, "Thank God that you only know this news. I don't like to tell you the other news. The enemy troops have crossed the borders, and they are heading for our village to besiege it. So, you ought to hide in the vault while I ascend to the roof with my gun to defend the house."

The woman almost died with fear. When they arrived home, she rushed to the vault and hid herself whereas her husband ascended to the rooftop with a shotgun in hand.

At night, the woman heard continuous gunshot and terrible noises shaking the house.

When the sounds of the battle finished, she was surprised by her husband who came in, raising his arm and shouting, "Thank God! I triumphed over the enemy!"

The next morning, the governor came and shouted at the peasant, "Where is the treasure you found? The whole of it is for me, as I am the governor of this village. Beware if you deny, your wife confessed everything before!"

The peasant couldn't help but laugh noisily and said, "Is it my wife who told you that? Don't you know that she is crazy? She is mentally handicapped."

The peasant called his wife who came, frightened. The moment she saw the governor holding a whip in his hand, she retold the whole story of the treasure adding that she had accompanied her husband to the town to conceal the treasure there.

The governor shook his head:

"When did this happen? Speak in front of your husband!"

"On the day of the great storm when it rained figs," the woman replied.

The man shouted, thinking that she was making fun of him. He ordered her to be polite in her reply.

She said, "I do not lie. All this took place on the day of the great battle when the enemy attacked the village, and my brave husband fought against the invaders all the night till he triumphed over them."

The man lost patience and shouted at her, "That's enough! What nonsense! Tell the truth. When did he take the treasure away to the town?"

The woman cried, "He went to the town on the day when the boss called you to pay the accounts, and you were screaming as the whips seared across your back!"

The governor flared up with rage and was persuaded of her madness. He seared her with his whip, and went away immediately, riding his horse.

The villagers noticed that the peasant disappeared on the other side of the country where he settled and started a new life as the richest man of his time.

References

'Handol and Doudol'

Hwan, Djuen Byeung and Hwang Il Yeung, 'Legendes des Monts Keumgang' in *Editions en Langues Etrangères*, North Korea, Pyong Yang, pp.87-95

'The Two Brothers'

n.a., ref. 'Les Deux Amies' in *Voice of Free China* magazine, vol.XXV, no.247, pp.7-9 and vol.XXV, no.248, pp.7-8

Address: *Voice of Free China* magazine, PO Box 24-38, Taipei, Taiwan

'The Treasure'

Ahmed, Nabila, *Al Arabi Assaghir* magazine, issue 22, pp.52-53

Address: *Al Arabi Assaghir* magazine, PO Box 748, Safat 13008, Kuwait

STONE C

THE STONE
THAT BINDS A COMMONWEALTH

BY

F. WALLACE CONNON

An extensive account of the Traditions, Historical Records and
Circumstantial Evidence concerning the Stone from earliest times
until the theft in 1950

INCLUDING A NEW CHAPTER ON

THE RETURN OF THE STONE TO
SCOTLAND

BY

MICHAEL A. CLARK

THE COVENANT PUBLISHING COMPANY LTD.
121, Low Etherley, Bishop Auckland, Co. Durham, DL14 0HA
2017

FIRST EDITION   1951
SECOND EDITION   2009
SECOND EDITION, revised   2017

Editorial Note

In reproducing the text for this edition the editorial team has attempted to identify Connon's sources and references. On the few occasions when we have been unable to do this we have, where possible, kept his statements but tried to include as much pertinent information as we can. This decision has been taken in order to retain the integrity of Connon's work.

ISBN 978-085205-069-9

CONTENTS

FOREWORD BY MICHAEL A. CLARK, 2009

WHEN the first edition of this volume was published in 1951, as Wallace Connon in his Preface records, the theft of the Coronation Stone was regarded as a sensational event. A group of four Scottish students took the Stone from Westminster Abbey on Christmas Day, 1950, to return it to Scotland. Thankfully it was recovered at Arbroath Abbey four months later and was in place for the Coronation of the Queen in 1953. This small volume subsequently became well known and for three decades it was regularly stocked by the Westminster Abbey Bookshop.

After the Government returned the Stone to Scotland in 1996 and on a visit to see the Stone, out of context and in a glass showcase in Edinburgh Castle, I spoke to the Guide on duty about the new book on the Stone that I had purchased – a very glossy production. He agreed it was well produced, but, he reflected, 'I still prefer the little red book they used to sell in the Westminster Abbey Bookshop.' He was quite moved to be told that he was speaking to the Chairman of the company that published the volume.

This new edition revives Wallace Connon's work, to which it is my privilege to add a new chapter on the constitutional significance of the return of the Stone to Scotland. A decade after that event, government papers were revealed which have great bearing on how the Royal Family and the Dean and Chapter of Westminster Abbey viewed the removal of such a sacred medieval artefact from the ancient Coronation Chair.

There is a far greater and wider appreciation of what the Stone of Destiny represents to the Realm than is generally realised and indeed, what it represents to our Covenant System of government, that of "The Queen-in-Parliament under God." We have, in the Stone, a symbol of the Stone Kingdom of God and of Jesus Christ, as the stone that the builders rejected, Who is destined to take up the throne of the Lord upon Earth.

At the present time a constitutional impasse is developing between the growing constitutional structures of the European Union and the British Constitution. The Stone of Destiny is at the very centre of this controversy. It is truly the Stone that binds a great Company and Commonwealth of Nations and it will yet be a symbol of their restored destiny, which is to lead the nations of the whole Earth in peace.

It is my fervent hope that this new edition will contribute to a far wider knowledge of where destiny should be directing us as a nation and people under God.

THE STONE OF DESTINY

PREFACE TO THE FIRST EDITION

THE sensational theft of the Coronation Stone, and the flood of inaccurate, misleading and cynical statements made concerning it in public comments following the event, call for as full a record of the history and traditions of the Stone as is possible with such a relic; for the public is always level-headed when it knows the full facts. Disraeli is credited with saying, 'A tradition can neither be made nor destroyed,' while Sir Arnold Wilson's definition is, 'Tradition is a sort of accumulated commonsense of centuries, a sort of balance to keep us on an even keel.' The facts on which a tradition is built may have become misrepresented with the passing of a long period of time, but always there is the foundation of fact which has acted as a warp for the design of the story, and however often the attempt is made to destroy the pattern with cynicism or scorn, the warp remains and resists all the wearing effects of both time and disbelief. Truth is often stranger than fiction, and the wise are never willing to discredit a tradition because of its disparity with generally accepted beliefs, nor are they willing to accept beliefs without carefully checking their origins.

The Coronation Stone, with its strange and fateful traditions, is a victim of this cynicism; yet, the implications of its traditions are so nationally important, and the ignorance of the majority of people concerning all the facts is so great, that it becomes necessary to record as many of them as possible.

It is not intended that this record should hide any discrepancies in the various traditions, nor find a solution for such differences; human nature and the passage of many centuries are bound to have left their mark. Neither does the record seek to prove the veracity of the ancient traditions concerning the Stone: there is no proof, as yet, otherwise there would be no mystery; likewise, there is no proof of their falsity. And so it is only right that all people should be aware of the historical facts, the traditions and the circumstantial evidence concerning this strange relic, in order to be able to decide for themselves the import of their story.

W.H. Stacpoole, LL.D., in his book *Coronation Regalia* quotes *The Archaeological Journal* of September 1856: 'One word more respecting the alleged antiquity of the stone, which Toland [1] does not hesitate to call "the ancientist respected monument in the world." In considering this question we are to try its claims to be what the traditions of the middle ages claim for it, by the same tests by which other reliques of high antiquity are tested. We are not to expect written evidence as we do for transactions of a time when the art of writing was extensively used, but *early traditional belief supported by parallel usages or incidents, and free from gross improbabilities.'* Stacpoole adds, 'And on such evidence he inclines to the belief that it came from the plains of Luz, and may be the very stone on which the patriarch Jacob rested his head.' [2]

We will take *The Archaeological Journal* as our example and copy its method; to it, and to the numerous writers from whose works I quote, I extend my grateful thanks.

F. WALLACE CONNON
March 1951

---

[1] JOHN TOLAND (1670 - 1722) was an Irish philosopher. He wrote *Christianity Not Mysterious* in 1696, and other books criticising ecclesiastical institutions.
[2] STACPOOLE, W.H. *Coronation Regalia: An Excursion into a Curious Bypath of Literature.* London: Whitaker's Almanack Office, 1911.

PART I   THE HISTORICAL SKELETON

CHAPTER I

THE TRADITIONS

ON April 9, 1946, the Ottawa correspondent of *The Times* reported:

'The Dominion Public Archive have to-day received from the Prime Minister, Mr. Mackenzie King, a document of historic interest and value – the plan of the hiding place of the Coronation Stone of Westminster Abbey during the war. The plan was forwarded for safe-keeping in the summer of 1940 through Sir Gerald Campbell, then High Commissioner of the United Kingdom in Canada. When, some months ago, war-time secrecy was lifted, Mr. Mackenzie King inquired, through Mr. Malcolm MacDonald, whether the document might not be allowed to remain in Canada, and the Dean of Westminster concurred.'[3]

The only information which the authorities at Westminster Abbey could be persuaded to release was that the Stone of Destiny 'did not leave the Abbey precincts,' that it was 'safe,' and that it would 'never have been discovered without the plan.'

Its hiding place remained a secret to the general public; only a small group of men high up in the affairs of State knew the secret, and, to provide against the possibility of the death of those resident in Britain who possessed that knowledge, a plan of the hiding place was placed in the hands of Mr. Mackenzie King, then Prime Minister of Canada, and it is this plan to which *The Times* report refers. Only after the theft of the Stone from the Abbey was it divulged that its war-time hiding place had been beneath the floor of the Islip Chapel.

The Stone was replaced under the seat of the Coronation Chair in the Sanctuary in Westminster Abbey late in 1945, and thus ended one of the historic acts in that great drama – the World War of 1939-45.

Mystery, drama, war. Were these conditions new or strange to the history of this Stone? Was this the first occasion that secrecy had torn it from its accepted place, 'The Sanctuary,' and transferred it to another, but always with the purpose of restoring it to the company of kings and priests?

---

[3] Ottawa Correspondent 'Coronation Stone's Hiding Place.' *The Times,* London, April 9, 1946.

One answer to these questions could be given by any one who interests themselves in these things; for, with the exception of certain necessary details, similar dramatic precautions for the safety and preservation of the Stone were taken during the war of 1914-18.

This previous, but still recent, historical proof of the veneration and guardianship bestowed on it, emphasises rather than answers the questions that arise: What mystery is hidden in the story of this rough stone which has been the seat of kings since the earliest records of our Island? Why, in this modern and materialistic age, when veneration seems to be a lost quality, and tradition the butt of the worldly wise, should the theft of the Stone have caused a feeling of deep tragedy?

If we take the *Westminster Abbey Guide* as our mentor we shall find the following description of the Stone:

'The Coronation Chair was made for Edward I to enclose the famous stone of Scone, which he seized in 1296, and brought from Scotland to the Abbey, where he placed it under the Abbot's care. The Scots made repeated and vain efforts to induce Edward to give it back. Tradition identifies this stone with the one upon which Jacob rested his head at Bethel: "And Jacob rose up early in the morning, and took the stone that he had put for his pillows, and set it up for a pillar, and poured oil upon the top of it" (*Genesis* 28:18). Jacob's sons carried it to Egypt, and from thence it passed to Spain with King Gathelus, son of Cecrops, the builder of Athens. About 700 BC it appears in Ireland, whither it was carried by the Spanish King's son Simon Brech, on his invasion of that Island. There it was placed upon the sacred hill of Tara, and called Lia-Fail, the "fatal" stone, or "stone of destiny," for when the Irish Kings were seated upon it at coronations the stone groaned aloud if the claimant was of Royal race, but remained silent if he was a pretender. Fergus II (d. 501), the founder of the Scottish monarchy and one of the Blood Royal of Ireland, received it in Scotland, and King Kenneth (d. 860) finally deposited it in the monastery of Scone (846). Setting aside the earlier myths, it is certain that it has been for centuries an object of veneration to the Scots, who fancied that "while it remained in their country, the State would be unshaken." Upon the stone their kings, down to John Balliol in 1292, were crowned, and it is said that the following distich had been engraved upon it by Kenneth:

Ni fallat fatum, Scoti quocunque locatum
Invenient lapidum regnare tenentur ibidem.
("If Fates go right, where'er this stone is found,
The Scots shall monarchs of that realm be found.")

– a prophecy which was fulfilled at the accession of James VI of Scotland and I of England.' [4]

In the *Official Souvenir Programme of 'The Coronation of Their Majesties King George VI and Queen Elizabeth'*, Sir Gerald Wollaston, Garter Principal King of Arms, in an article headed 'The Coronation Ceremony,' states:

'A word may here be said of that most venerable relic, King Edward's Chair. It is made of oak of an architectural design, the feet being formed of four sejant lions, and is attributed to contain a far more ancient and famous object, known as the stone of Scone, which forms its seat. It is a block of reddish sandstone and, if the legends about it are to be believed, is the stone on which the Patriarch Jacob laid his head at Bethel, its subsequent migrations ending in its removal from Spain to Ireland by Simon Brech, who was crowned upon it there 700 years before the Christian era. There certainly was a stone corresponding to it in Ireland, preserved on the Hill of Tara, possibly as a stone used for purposes of consecration in that country. The Irish called it the Stone of Destiny, due to its alleged power of emitting an oracular sound to show the legitimacy of Royal descent. It may well have been taken from Ireland to the West of Scotland, early in the Christian era, by the settlers from Ireland who established themselves in that country, for it certainly existed in that part of Scotland long before the ninth century, when it was removed by King Kenneth from Dunstaffnage to the Abbey of Scone. In Scotland the stone was accorded the same veneration, including the tradition that its possession was essential to the preservation of regal power. At Scone all Kings of Scotland were crowned upon it until the year 1296, when Edward I brought it to England and left it as an

---

[4] BRADLEY, E.T. & M.C. *The Westminster Abbey Guide*. 34th ed. London: Jarrold & Sons Ltd, 1959. pp.101-102.

offering of conquest at the Shrine of Edward the Confessor in Westminster Abbey.'[5]

These are official records of the traditions attached to the Stone, but there is one other tradition which we must add to complete the story, and which ought not to be omitted, for it is held by the Masonic Craft whose history and symbolism go back as far as the Stone itself. It is to be found in *The Encyclopaedia of Freemasonry* by Waite:

'MARK MASONRY – *The Stone of Destiny:*
'(I) On this stone stood the Angel with flaming sword to keep the way of Paradise, when Adam and Eve were expelled.
'(II) It formed the top of the altar raised by Abraham for the sacrifice of his son Isaac.
'(III) It was the Pillar of Jacob when he had his vision of the ladder.
'(IV) Innumerable attempts were made to place it in one position and another during the building of the first temple, but it found no rest anywhere until it became the capstone.
'(V) It was saved from destruction with the Temple, was cherished as a palladium by the Jews; and, after the death of Zedekiah, was carried by a migrating colony, with "Scota the King's daughter" under the leadership of the prophet Jeremiah.
'(VI) It was taken to "The Isles of the Sea", and preserved as a Stone of Destiny, by the "People of Scota".
'(VII) Finally, it was "stolen" by Edward, King of England, and placed in the Coronation Chair at Westminster Abbey where it still is.'[6]

In his book, *Historical Memorials of Westminster Abbey*, Dean Stanley, one-time custodian of the Stone, sums up its historical importance with these words:

'It is the one primeval monument which binds together the whole Empire. The iron rings, the battered surface, the crack which has all but rent its solid mass asunder, bear witness to its long migrations. It is thus embedded in the heart of the English monarchy – an element of poetic, patriarchal, heathen times, which, like Araunah's rocky threshing floor in the midst of the

[5] King George's Jubilee Trust. *Official Souvenir Programme of The Coronation of Their Majesties King George VI and Queen Elizabeth*. London: Odhams Press Ltd, 1937. pp. 19-20.
[6] WAITE, A.E. *The Encyclopaedia of Freemasonry*. London: W. Rider & Son, 1921. Vol. ii, p. 37.

Temple of Solomon, carries back our thoughts to races and customs now almost extinct; a link which unites the Throne of England to the traditions of Tara and Iona.'[7]

In order to obtain a clear idea of the various and sometimes conflicting claims set out in these traditions, let us correlate them and then deal with each one separately.

   I   It is composed of red sandstone.
  II   It has an iron ring at each end.
 III   It is the stone on which Jacob rested his head at Bethel.
 IV   It was carried to Egypt by Jacob's sons.
  V   It came under the care of King Gathelus.
 VI   It came under the care of Scota, the daughter of Pharaoh.
 VII   It was taken to Spain.
VIII   It was taken to Ireland.
 IX   It was placed at Tara.
  X   It became a capstone of the Temple at Jerusalem, but was saved from destruction with the Temple and carried by a migrating colony under Jeremiah.
 XI   It was removed from Ireland to Scotland.
 XII   It was taken to Westminster Abbey by Edward I.

The claims that it was the stone on which the angel stood when expelling Adam and Eve from Eden, and that it was the top of the altar raised by Abraham for the sacrifice of his son Isaac, must be left to the Masonic Craft to deal with in their secret traditions: it would not be in order to discuss their findings here, and there is no historical tradition or biblical record suggesting these points.

Before examining these various claims, let us examine ourselves, for our outlook in these days on matters that cannot be proved by demonstration is frequently inconsistent. We accept without demur scientific statements which are, as yet, but theories based on deduction from ascertained facts; we accept freely anthropological verdicts estimating the ages of skeletons which have been unearthed as hundreds of thousands, and even millions of years; we are ready to believe that our ancestors in these Islands were 'painted savages' before the coming of the Romans, although our authoritative historians and antiquarians have told us otherwise; the theory of evolution is generally accepted although no

---

[7]STANLEY, A. P. *Historical Memorials of Westminster Abbey*, 2nd ed. London: John Murray, 1868. p.66.

authoritative scientist can claim complete proof for the theory, and many of high repute completely reject it; yet, when we come to deal with a matter where the spiritual is claimed to impinge on the physical, and where biblical history and prophecy find their place, we become not only critical, which is wise, but cynical, which is unwise.

Winston S. Churchill, the unrivalled statesman and historian, in his essay on Moses, included in his book, *Thoughts and Adventures*, takes his stand firmly on the side of these ancient records:

> 'We believe that the most scientific view, the most up-to-date and rationalistic conception, will find its fullest satisfaction in taking the Bible story literally...We may be sure that all these things happened just as they are set out according to Holy Writ. We may believe that they happened to people not so very different from ourselves, and that the impressions those people received were faithfully recorded, and have been transmitted across the centuries with far more accuracy than many of the telegraphed accounts we read of the goings-on of today...Let the men of science and of learning expand their knowledge and probe with their researches every detail of the records which have been preserved to us from these dim ages. All they will do is to fortify the grand simplicity and essential accuracy of the recorded truths which have lighted so far the pilgrimage of man.' [8]

Let us remember as we proceed that we are not weaving a romance with the Stone as the 'hero' of the story, but endeavouring to piece together the mosaic of secular history, circumstantial evidence, tradition and biblical prophecy and history which are embodied in the records already quoted, and to answer the wholly reasonable question: Why was the loss of the Stone regarded at the time by most people as a national tragedy?

Let us go back over the centuries, gathering the bones of the facts in an effort to form the skeleton of the mystery of the Stone, and then clothe it with as many reasonable deductions as circumstantial evidence will allow.

---

[8] CHURCHILL, WINSTON S. *Thoughts and Adventures*. London: Odhams, 1947. pp. 293-294.

CHAPTER II

THE CLAIMS

(I)   The Stone is composed of red sandstone

IN articles and letters published in the Press following the theft of the Stone from Westminster Abbey, the assertion was repeatedly made that it was quarried in Scotland – although the authorities quoted express widely differing opinions as to the exact locality of its origin. There are a number of records of examination of the Stone by experts:

- in *Historical Memorials of Westminster Abbey* Dean Stanley cites the report of an analysis in 1865 by the late professor A. C. Ramsay, LL.D., F.R.S., Director of the Geological Survey of England; [9]
- a letter from Sir Archibald Geikie, the noted geologist who examined the Stone, is quoted by W. F. Skene in *The Coronation Stone*; [10]
- and in an article in *The Illustrated London News* of January 13, 1951, C. F. Davidson, D.Sc., F.R.S.E., sets out the opinions he reached as a result of a geological examination of the Stone.

Each of these experts has been careful to make it clear that nothing has been absolutely proved concerning the origin of the Stone:

'...It may be impossible to prove precisely its origin' (Ramsay); '...There is no clue in the stone itself to fix precisely its original source' (Geikie);   '...Its lithological character is such that it has always been found a difficult matter to trace it with any certainty to the locality whence it was derived' (Davidson).

The obstinate fact remains that, even if stone of the same type has been found in one country, not until there is proof that such stone is unobtainable in any of the other countries mentioned in the traditions is the source of the Stone established.

---

[9] STANLEY, op.cit. p.564.
[10] SKENE, WILLIAM F. *The Coronation Stone*, p. 50, taken from '*Proceedings of the Society*', Archaeological Data Society Journal, March 8, 1869. p.81.

13

Until recent years it was believed that the rock formations in Palestine are all of limestone; and a statement by Professor Ramsay that the Stone was of calcareous sandstone, unlikely to have come from Bethel, since 'according to all credible reports' the rocks around that area 'are formed of strata of limestone,' has been widely quoted.

Such is an opinion held in the last century, but we now have a Palestinian Government publication of 1935, written by its Geological Advisor, G. S. Blake, B.Sc. A.R.S.M., F.G.S., M.I.M.M., and bearing the title, *The Stratigraphy of Palestine and its Building Stones.* The following are a few extracts from this report:

Part I. Stratigraphy:
p.5. Gaza Coastal Plain and Beersheba District:
'In the Gaza district where the ridges have been eroded there is always exposed a sandstone core.'

p.6. North of Gaza:
'...the ridges may consist partly or wholly of consolidated sandstone.'

p.9. Jaffa – Haifa:
'Between Caesarea and Haifa the single ridge is a highly calcareous sandstone.'

p.15. Inland:
'...conglomerates with basalt pebbles overlain with calcareous sandstone which is almost quartz-free.'

p.19. The Jordan Valley:
'The Upper Pliocene consists of sandstone overlain with conglomerates...'

p.51. In Transjordan:
'...where the upturned edges of the Turonian and Cenomamian limestone come up against Nubian sandstone...'

p.78. Dead Sea:
'...there is a formation of red sandstone.'

Part II. Building Stones:

p.98. Sandstone:

'True sandstones occur only in the Nubian or lower beds. In Northern Palestine soft sandstones and ferruginous hard sandstones occur exposed in a few localities, such as Wadi Farah and Hula, but are not used, and are probably of little value as building stones.'

p.98. Calcareous Sandstone:

'Most of the sandstone quarries...occur on the ridge between Atlit and Tantura' (on the coastal plain).

p.100. Siliceous Rocks:

'In the Jordan Valley, there exists a sandstone of Pliocene age, which directly overlies beds of Cretaceous age. Good examples occur forming the top of the round hill to the south of Km.31, and there is a long outcrop at Khirbet es Simrah north of Jericho... Like the sandstone of the coastal plain it is highly calcareous...'[11]

These geological reports do not prove that the Stone came from the Palestinian area, but they do at least show that the possibility of it having come from there must be taken into consideration when investigating its traditions.

(II)   It has an iron ring at each end

Why iron rings if not as a means of carrying the Stone? Dean Stanley in his *Historical Memorials of Westminster Abbey* declares:

'The iron rings, the battered surface, the crack which has all but rent its solid mass asunder, bear witness to its long migrations.'[12]

There has, however, been no need for many, or even long migrations since its arrival in Ireland, Scotland or England; for in each of these

---

[11]BLAKE, G.S. *The Stratigraphy of Palestine and its Building Stones.* Palestine Government Stationery Office, 1935. Available from The Palestine Exploration Fund Organisation.
[12] STANLEY, op.cit. p.66.

countries it remained for centuries as the crowning seat of kings, and was only removed direct from one place to the next. Some writers suggest that the rings were fixed for its removal from Scotland to England, but surely the victorious army of Edward I had some form of horse transport capable of carrying a three-hundredweight stone; even Boadicea, a thousand years earlier, had chariots. It would seem, therefore, but logical to look further and earlier for more migrations, and more continuous movement. The traditions claim Spain, Egypt and Palestine.

(III) It is the stone on which Jacob rested his head when he had the vision at Bethel

The 1935 report of the Geological Advisor to the Palestine Government on *The Stratigraphy of Palestine and its Building Stones* [13] indicates the possibility of its having come from the locality of Bethel. The only book that gives any record of Jacob's stone, or even any hints that it may have been preserved, is the Bible, and thus to it we must turn.

> *Genesis* 28: 'And he dreamed, and behold a ladder set up on the earth, and the top of it reached to heaven: and behold the angels of God ascending and descending on it. And, behold, the LORD stood above it, and said, I am the LORD God of Abraham thy father, and the God of Isaac: the land whereon thou liest, to thee will I give it, and to thy seed; And thy seed shall be as the dust of the earth, and thou shalt spread abroad to the west, and to the east, and to the north, and to the south: and in thee and in thy seed shall all the families of the earth be blessed. And, behold, I am with thee, and will keep thee in all places whither thou goest, and will bring thee again into this land; for I will not leave thee, until I have done that which I have spoken to thee of (vv.12-15).
>
> 'And Jacob rose up early in the morning, and took the stone that he had put for his pillows, and set it up for a pillar, and poured oil upon the top of it (v.18).
>
> 'And Jacob vowed a vow, saying... This stone, which I have set for a pillar, shall be God's house: and of all that thou shalt give me I will surely give the tenth unto thee (v.22).'

---

[13] BLAKE, op.cit.

A WITNESS TO GOD'S PROMISES

Whatever the modern cynics may think about the dream, Jacob himself had no doubt about its significance – that his people would spread to the four corners of the earth – and as a continual symbol of its fulfilment he set up and anointed with oil that Stone which was to continue to be 'God's House,' and a witness that all God had promised him would come to pass.

There is no record of what Jacob did with the Stone, but it is hardly likely that he who had had such a dream, and believed its import, would leave it lying just where he 'set it up'; it is more likely that, at the earliest opportunity, he secured its safe-keeping as an heirloom for generations to come, the seed that were to be 'as the dust of the earth.'

It is sometimes forgotten that, as recorded, Jacob visited Bethel a second time:

> *Genesis* 35: 'And God said unto Jacob, Arise, go up to Bethel, and dwell there: and make there an altar unto God, that appeared unto thee when thou fleddest from the face of Esau thy brother (v.1)...So Jacob came to Luz, (Bethel), and he built there an altar (vv. 6,7)...And God appeared unto Jacob again...and blessed him. And God said unto him, Thy name is Jacob: thy name shall not be called any more Jacob, but Israel shall be thy name: and he called his name Israel (vv. 9,10)...And God said unto him, I am God Almighty: be fruitful and multiply; a nation and a company of nations shall be of thee, and kings shall come out of thy loins (v. 11)...And Jacob set up a pillar in the place where he talked with him, even a pillar of stone...and he poured oil thereon (v. 14).'

This time it was a command from God to go to Bethel and again set up an altar to Him as he had done on his first visit. Is it not a reasonable suggestion that he used for this second occasion the same 'pillar of stone' as when at Bethel the previous time he had received his first promise from God? This time it was promised that his seed was to become a 'nation and a company of nations.' These records, as yet, only bring out the importance of the Stone to Jacob and his descendants, and the veneration which must have been bestowed on it as a symbol of their future greatness. The claimed migrations had not yet begun.

(IV) It was carried to Egypt by Jacob's sons

Only a few years after Jacob's second visit to Bethel his son Joseph was sold into bondage in Egypt and eventually became next in authority to Pharaoh. Having been visited by his brothers, when they journeyed to Egypt to buy corn during the seven years' famine, he persuaded his father, Jacob, and his brothers to settle there, and received from Pharaoh permission for them to dwell in Goshen.

Nearly twenty years later Jacob felt that he was near his death, and called all his sons before him that he might bless each of them before he died: 'That I may tell you that which shall befall you in the last days.' His blessing and prophecy concerning Joseph was:

> *Genesis* 49:22-24: 'Joseph is a fruitful bough, even a fruitful bough by a well; whose branches run over the wall. The archers have sorely grieved him, and shot at him, and hated him: but his bow abode in strength, and the arms of his hands were made strong by the hands of the mighty God of Jacob; (from thence is the shepherd, the stone of Israel).'

Like many other biblical passages the meaning of these concluding words is not clear, and none of the commentators can claim that his suggestions concerning them are fully satisfactory.

ISRAEL'S GUARDIAN STONE

What was 'the stone of Israel'? Surely it was the stone which Jacob, who by then was renamed Israel, had used when he received his vision and the far-reaching promises for his future seed. One translator, Ferrar Fenton, renders it, 'from whom is Israel's guardian stone'; and so it may be that Jacob, having carried it with him to Egypt, wished, before he died, to ensure that its safe keeping was transferred to the hands of his illustrious and powerful son, Joseph, whose seed 'in the last days' were to spread far from their home land, 'run over the wall,' and to be hated and attacked by their enemies.

The *Chronicon Rhythmicum*, in *Chronicles of the Scots*,[14] by W. F. Skene, LL.D., uses, when dealing with the story of the Stone, the words

---

[14] SKENE, W.F. ed. *Chronicles of the Picts, Chronicles of the Scots and other Early Memorials of Scottish History.* Edinburgh: H.M. General Register House, 1867.

lapidem Pharaonis, namely, Pharaoh's stone from Egypt, (the same expression is quoted in Johannes de Fordun's *Scotichronicon* [15]); also in *A Critical Essay on the Ancient Inhabitants of the Northern Parts of Britain or Scotland,* [16] by Thomas Innes: they occur in the sections headed *Gaithelos Intulit Lapidem.*

(V) It came under the care of King Gathelus

(VI) It came under the care of Scota the daughter of Pharaoh

The Chronicles of Scotland by Hector Boece (translated into Scots by John Bellenden, 1531), tells us that the ancestor of the Scots was 'ane Greyk callit Gathelus, son of Cecrops of Athens, utherwayis of Argus, King of Argives,' who came to Egypt when 'in this tyme rang (reigned) in Egypt Pharo ye scurge of ye pepill of Israell.' Gethelus gained a great victory for Pharo against 'the Moris and pepill of Ynde' and 'King pharo gaif him his dochter, callit Scota, in marriage.' [17]

According to *The Harmsworth Encyclopaedia,* [18] Cecrops was the mythical founder of Athens and its first king, and was thought to be originally a leader of a band of colonists from Egypt.

Boece, and other early historians, may have gathered their information from earlier records which were extant in their time, but have since been lost. Similarly, Sir William Bentham, Ulster King-of-Arms, suggests in his *Etruria – Celtica:*

'The written histories by the Britons themselves, which may have existed, did not survive the Roman conquest; it was the policy of those conquerors to obliterate, as much as possible, the origin of the people they subjected to their yoke. That they did write is certain, for Caesar tells us the Britons were more learned than the Gauls – a strong proof that the Gauls and Britons of Caesar's day were a literate and well-informed people, and not a

[15] GOODALL, WALTER. ed. Johannes de Fordun: *Scotichronicon.* Edinburgh, 1759.

[16] INNES, THOMAS, *A Critical Essay on the Ancient Inhabitants of the Northern Parts of Britain, or Scotland.* London: William Innes, 1729. p. 426.

[17] BOECE, HECTOR, *Scotorum historiae a prima gentis origine* (*The History and Chronicles of Scotland*). 1527. Translated by Bellenden. Paris, 1536. Vol. i, pp. 21-27. John Bellenden was appointed by King James V to translate it into the Scottish vernacular; the translation appeared in 1536.

[18] HAMMERTON, J.A. ed. *The Harmsworth Encyclopaedia ('Everybody's book of reference').* 9 vols. London: The Amalgamated Press Ltd., 1922-3.

set of ignorant and unimproved barbarians, as had been asserted.' [19]

But there is no conclusive proof of Boece's statements, the only helpful evidence being that several ancient writers claim the Greeks of that period as Israelites, and later writers claim the existence in Spain of colonies of the same people.

THE DANAUS LEGEND

For example, Muller, in the *Fragmenta Historicorum Graecorum*, writes of the literary sources of the Danaus legend, which appear to be largely in the works of Hecataeus of Abdera, a fourth-century BC Greek historian, and Diodorus of Sicily who copied from him:

> 'Hecataeus, therefore, tells us that the Egyptians, formerly, being troubled by calamities, in order that the divine wrath might be averted, expelled all the aliens gathered together in Egypt. Of these, some, under their leaders Danaus and Cadmus, migrated to Greece.' [20]

The 'calamities' referred to were obviously the plagues which Moses was commanded by God to bring upon Egypt, and the 'aliens' were the Israelites, some of whom migrated to Greece with Danaus and Cadmus, while the remainder, under the leadership of Moses, trekked to the Wilderness of Sinai.

The Diodorus version of the story is as follows:

> 'Now the Egyptians say that also after these events a great number of colonies were spread from Egypt all over the inhabited world... They say also that those who set forth with Danaus, likewise from Egypt, settled what is practically the oldest city of Greece, Argos, and that the nations of the Colchi in Pontus and that of the Jews, which lies between Arabia and Syria, were founded as colonies by certain emigrants from their country; and this is the reason why it is a long-established institution among these two peoples to circumcise their male

---

[19] BENTHAM, SIR WILLIAM, *Etruria Celtica - Etruscan literature and antiquities investigated.* 2 volumes. Dublin: Philip Dixon Hardy & Sons, 1842. p.3.
[20] MÜLLER, C. & F. *Fragmenta Historicorum Graecorum.* 5 vols. Paris, 1841–7. Vol. ii, p. 385.

children, the custom having been brought over from Egypt. Even the Athenians, they say, are colonists from Sais in Egypt.' [21]

Dr. R. G. Latham, the ethnologist, asserts:

'Neither do I think that the eponymus of the Argive Danai was other than that of the Israelites tribe of Dan; only we are so used to confine ourselves to the soil of Palestine in our consideration of the history of the Israelites, that we treat them as if they were *adscripti glebae*, and ignore the share they may have taken in the ordinary history of the world.' [22]

So, it would seem, the Stone could still be in the hands of the sons of Jacob when in the care of Gathelus and his Queen Scota.

(VII) It was taken to Spain

The Chronicles of Scotland, by Hector Boece, continues the story of Gathelus, who is said to have left Egypt with his wife (Scota), his friends and a company of Greeks and Egyptians rather than 'to abyde ye manifest wengeance of goddis,' which the plagues of Egypt demonstrated, and, travelling by the sea, 'callit Mediterrane,' 'efter lang tyme he landit in ane part of Spayne callit Lusitan,' later called Potingall. After this he built the city of Brigance and 'callit his subdittis (subjects) Scottis in honour and affeccioun of his wyiff.' And, peace having been secured, 'Gathelus sittand in his chayr of merbell within his citie.' This chair of marble had such fortune and omen that wherever it was found in any land the same land shall become the native land of the Scots.

'The Scottis sall ioyis and brouke the landis haill Quhair yai fynd it, bot gif weirdis faill.'
(Translation: 'The Scots shall brook that realm as native ground if words fail not, where'er this chair is found.') [23]

It should be noted that *The Students' English Dictionary* defines 'marble' as 'any species of calcareous stone susceptible of a good polish.'

[21] DIODORUS SICULUS. *Bibliotheca Historica*. Trans. C.H. Oldfather , Cambridge, MA: Harvard University Press, 1935. Book I, chapter ii.
[22] LATHAM, R.G. *Ethnology of Europe*. London: John Van Voorst, 1852. p.37.
[23] BOECE, op.cit.

JEWISH COLONIES IN SPAIN

Isaac da Costa (1798-1860), a Dutch theologian and doctor of law and literature, was of Jewish parentage, but became a director of a seminary which was part of the mission of the Free Church of Scotland. The following is an extract from his work, *Israel and the Gentiles*:

'The wholly exceptional standing of these Sephardim (South European) Jews is explained by both Jewish and Spanish writers of the Peninsula as being due to the ancient tradition of their descent from the House of David, or from the Royal stem of Judah at any rate. The persistent maintenance of this tradition even by Spanish authors, who are by no means to be accused of partiality to the Jews (at least in regard to faith), is certainly most remarkable. Don Jose Amador de Los Rios, in his important work, *Estudios Historicos, Politicos y Literarios sobre los Judios de Espana* (Madrid, 1848), constantly refers to the Spanish Jews as being descended from David and the house of Judah.' [24]

More will be said of the settlement of the Jews in Spain in a later section.

(VIII)   It was later taken to Ireland

The Chronicles of Scotland continues the record of Gathelus and his descendants thus: 'Ane certaine of this pepill be process of tyme' was sent to Ireland. In due course Symon Breck, a descendant of Gathelus, was sent for by the Scots in Ireland to become their king, and he was received with great solemnity, 'and efter crownit with princelie dignite in ye chayr of merbell, quhilk (which) he brocht with him furth of Spanye.' 'This Symon was ye furst King that rang abone (reigned over) ye Scottis in Ireland.' Boece gives the period as 'fra ye begynnyng of Rome LX yeris; before the Incarnacioun of God VIc LXXXXV yeris,' namely, six centuries and 95 years, or 695 BC. [25]

The History of Scotland, in Latin, by George Buchanan, gives the following information:

[24] DA COSTA, ISAAC: *Israel and the Gentiles*. Trans. M. Kennedy, in *Noble Families Among the Sephardic Jews*, 14th edn. Ed. B. Brewster. Oxford: Oxford University Press/Humphrey Milford, 1936. Vol.3. p.970.
[25] BOECE, op.cit. pp. 21, 27.

'I now commence with the universal report, which is confirmed by a number of proofs, that a colony of Spaniards, either driven from home by their more powerful neighbours, or emigrating voluntarily with their superabundant progeny, transported themselves into Ireland, and took possession of the coast of that Island which lay nearest to them... In the meantime, while the Scots, for that was the name of the whole people...' [26]

THE HARP OF DAVID

An interesting sidelight is to be found in the *Dialogo della Musica Antica*, where Vincenzio de Galilei mentions that the harp of Ireland owes its origin to the Harp of David:

'This most ancient instrument (commemorated Dante) was brought to us from Ireland where such are most excellently worked and in a great number; the inhabitants of the said island have made this their art during the many centuries they have lived there and, moreover, it is a special undertaking of the kingdom; and they paint and engrave it in their public and private buildings and on their hill; stating as their reason for so doing that they have descended from the Royal Prophet David.' [27]

'OLLAM FOLA' – 'THE WONDERFUL PROPHET'

The Annals of the Four Masters (translation and notes by O'Conor), indicates some link between the Israelite colonists and Ireland, for it is not usual for a country to include a foreigner in a gallery of its famous men unless he had some affinity with their own heroes.

'Ollam Fola is celebrated in ancient history as a sage and legislator, eminent for learning, wisdom and excellent institutions, and his historic frame has been recognised by placing his medallion in *basso relievo* with those of Moses and other great legislators in the interior of the dome of the Four Courts of Dublin... The ancient Records and Chronicles of the Kingdom were ordered to be written and carefully preserved at Tara by

[26] BUCHANAN, GEORGE. *Rerum Scoticarum Historia* (*The History of Scotland*). Trans. James Aikman. Glasgow: Blackie, Fullarton & Co., 1827. Vol.i, book iv, pp. 150-4. Buchanan was Director of the Chancery during the Regency of the Earl of Moray; Lord Privy Seal during the Regency of the Earl of Lennox; and also tutor to young King James VI.
[27] GALILEI, VINCENZIO. *Dialogo della musica antica e moderna... in sua difesa contro Ioseffo Zerlino*. Florence: Filippo Giunti, 1581.

Ollam Fola and there formed the basis of the Ancient History of Ireland, called the Psalter of Tara.' [28]

Another translation, called *Annals of the Kingdom of Ireland by the Four Masters*, edited from *MSS* in the Library of the Royal Irish Academy and of Trinity College, Dublin (translation and notes by John O'Donovan, M.T.I.A.), gives:

'Ollamh Fodhla after having been forty years in the sovereignty of Ireland died at his own house at Teamhair... Eochaidh was the first name of Ollamh Fodhla; and he was called Ollamh because he had been first a learned Ollamh, and afterwards king (Fodhla) of Ireland.' [29]

EMBLEMS IN IMITATION OF THE TWELVE TRIBES
In the Library of the Royal Irish Academy there is a *MS* translation from the Irish of a poem entitled, *The Kings of the Race of Eibhear*; it is to be found in Dr. Geoffrey Keating's *Foras Feasa ar Eirinn* (translation by David Comyn), and is introduced by these words:

'It is a long time since the Gaels began the practice of having emblems, in imitation of the Children of Israel, who employed them in Egypt, in the lifetime of Gaedheal, when the Children of Israel passed through the Red Sea, with Moses as their chief leader. Now there were twelve tribes of them and each tribe had a separate division of an army and a separate emblem.' [30]

Then follows a list of the emblems of the twelve tribes of Israel, and the poem giving a verse to each tribe.

There is another translation of the poem by Michael Kearney (1635-65), who is the earliest known English versifier of Irish poetry; it is also in the Royal Irish Academy, being among the collection made by William

[28] O'CONOR, CHARLES. trans. *Rerum Hibernicarum scriptores veteres iii: Quatuor Magistrorum Annales Hibernici usque ad annum M.CLXXII. ex ipso O'Clerii autographo in Biblioteca Stowense servato, nunc primum uersione donati ac notis illustrate.* London:Buckingham. 1826. p. 297. Notes by O'Conor. NB: the dome of the Four Courts of Dublin was destroyed in the Civil War of 1922.
[29] O'DONOVAN. ed. and trans. *Annála Ríoghachta Eireann (The Annals of the Four Masters)* 6 vols. Dublin, 1856. M3922.1 and M3922.3 Vol. i, pp. 53-5.
[30] KEATING, GEOFFREY *Foras Feasa ar Éirinn (The History of Ireland.)* 4 vols. Eds. D. Comyn, &. P.S. Dineen. London: Irish Texts Society, 1902-14. Vol. iii, pp. 125, 126.

Elliott Hudson whose library was bequeathed to that institution. The introduction reads:

> 'The Vse of Armes and Escouchions is anciently obserued by the Irishry, in imitation of ye Children of Israell, who began to vse them in Egypt (at which time the Ancestor of all the Irishry, called Gaoidhil, or Gathelus, there liued), which Armes, the Israellits at their passing through ye Redd Seas, vnder the conduct of Moyses, did carry in their seuerall Banners. They were in all Twelue Tribes, and each Tribe had a certaine number of men under his own command with Distinct Banners and Armes.'

Then follows the list of banners of the tribes of Israel. It continues:

> 'And that these Armes formerly mentioned were those which the children of Israell did beare in their Banners, it is warranted by an ancient Irish Rhyme extant in the olde booke of Leackine in Ormond within the Country of Tipperary, which Rhyme in Irish, and translated into English, Disticke for Disticke, is as followeth...' [31]

Then follows the poem giving a verse to each tribe.

These extracts, with the exception of the one from Boece, make no reference to the Stone, but they do refer to the settlement in Ireland of a people from Spain who show great interest in the history of the original guardians of the Stone, and, indeed, claim descent from them. However, James Anderson, D.D., in his *Royal Genealogies*, [32] gives the descent of ancient Irish kings and couples Simeon Breac with the 'fatal stone.'

(IX) It was placed at Tara

Tamar was a name which we find among the daughters of the Royal House of Israel (II *Samuel* 13:1), the House of David, and if the claim of the Irish to be descended from that line is correct we need not be surprised to find the name Tamar in their records.

In the *Annals of the Kingdom of Ireland by the Four Masters*, appears the following statement:

---

[31] JOHN O'DUGAN (c. 1370). *The Kings of the Race of Eibhear*. Trans. Michael Kearney, 1635.
[32] ANDERSON, JAMES. *Royal Genealogies*. London: James Bettenham, 1732. p. 775.

'Tea, daughter of Lughaidh, son of Ith, whom Eremhon married in Spain, to the repudiation of Odhbha, was the Tea who requested of Eremhon a choice hill, as her dower, in whatever place she should select it, that she might be interred therein, and that her mound and her gravestone might be thereon raised, and where every prince ever to be born of her race should dwell. The guarantees who undertook to execute this for her were Amhergin Gluingeal and Emhear Finn. The hill she selected was Druim Caein, i.e. Teamhair. It is from her it was called, and in it was she interred.'[33]

Then follows a footnote by O'Donovan: 'The dower was a reward always given by the husband to the wife, at their marriage, a custom which prevailed among the Jews, and is still observed by the Turks and other eastern nations.'

DERIVATION OF THE WORD TARA

The Rev. Duncan McDougall, M.A., formerly Examiner in Hebrew for the Free Church College, Edinburgh, and McPherson Scholar in Celtic Language and Literature, Edinburgh, has given permission to quote from a letter to the author:

'To the ordinary reader the word Tara means exactly nothing. "The harp that once through Tara's halls, the soul of music shed" leaves them under the impression that Tara was a place, somewhere in Ireland; but there never was a place in Ireland of that name.

'"Tara," a name so familiar to English-speaking people, contains within it a proof which is highly important; the story of Tamar-Tephi is very often pooh-poohed as an ancient fable, unworthy of credence. Where is the proof? In the word "Tara." "Tara" is the English corruption of the Irish word commonly written "Teamhara," which is the genitive of Teamhar or Tamar. The final "a" has been aspirated according to the Hebrew rule of aspiration, which in Irish has been extended to apply to the letter "m." In this form it almost disappears, making a sound like "Tea-wra," which to English ears became "Tara."

'It is important to note that what we call "Tara" is the genitive of "Tamar," and being a genitive it never stands alone; it must be

---

[33] O'DONOVAN, op.cit. M3502.2. Vol. i, p. 31.

governed in the genitive by another noun. Thus the great palace of Ulster, designed by Queen Tamar, which embodied a form of Architecture which made it for centuries the wonder of Ireland, was called simply "Tigh Teamhara," "The House of Tamar."

'It is this title which has become to the poet "Tara's Halls." The hill on which the palace stood is known in Irish history as "Cnoc Teamhara," "the Hill of Tamar"; and, as all Irish legislation was enacted there, it is the nearest that Irish history knows to "Tara" as "the ancient capital of Ireland."

'Thus reasoning from the known to the unknown, we begin with the familiar word "Tara," and we find that Tara is an English corruption of an Irish genitive of a Hebrew woman's name – Tamar. There was one other thing to which the name Tamar stands for ever attached, which aroused the awe and admiration of the Irish even more than the palace which she built; that was the harp which was her most precious heirloom, which appears to have been proof of her Royal lineage, "the harp that once through Tamar's halls, the soul of music shed." What the kings of Ireland thought of that harp is demonstrated in the fact that they placed it on the Royal Standard, and there it stands to this day to prove that the story of Tamar is no myth.'

The Stone, which, from the time of King Gathelus, seemed to have become the personal heirloom of their Kings, would, naturally, find its refuge, when in Ireland, in the Palace of Queen Tamar, i.e. 'Tigh Teamhara' – 'The House of Tamar.'

(X) It became the capstone of the Temple at Jerusalem, but was saved from destruction with the Temple, and carried by a migrating colony under Jeremiah

If the Stone was taken from Egypt by Gathelus at the time of the plagues, then it could not have been with the remainder of the Israelites during their wanderings in the Wilderness, and later have become a capstone of the Temple at Jerusalem. This, however, does not mean that either tradition is entirely wrong, for, chronologically, they meet again in the next stage, during the period of Simon Brech and Jeremiah whose lives touched part of the same century: both traditions agree that its guardians were the 'people of Scota,' and its destination 'the isles of the

27

sea'; the Masonic tradition omits Spain and substitutes the Temple at Jerusalem.

ISRAELITISH VENERATION FOR A STONE

In our search for circumstantial evidence, or, as the *Archaeological Journal* puts it, 'early traditional belief supported by parallel usages or incidents,' we can turn to one book only, the Bible. There we find several occasions during the history of the Israelites, between Egypt and the Temple, when a special stone is mentioned. Moreover, if the precious heirloom of Jacob-Israel was handed over to Joseph for custody, then, as he took an oath of the Children of Israel saying, 'God will surely visit you, and ye shall carry up my bones from hence' (*Genesis* 50:24, 25), it would be a natural act to take with them the Stone of which he was custodian.

It is a frailty of human nature that something tangible is needed by most people as a symbol to help them to realise the 'presence' of the spiritual in their lives; it is unfortunate that the symbol sometimes eventually takes the place of the spiritual truth which it represents, and is treated as an object of veneration and worship in itself.

This may have been the case with the Children of Israel and the Stone: for Jeremiah (2:27) upbraids them for their idolatry in these words: 'Saying to a stock, Thou art my father; and to a stone, Thou hast brought me forth.' It would seem as if they had some stone which they had preserved and come to revere as a sacred relic; and, remembering their wonderful past deliverance from the Egyptians at the Red Sea, had perhaps looked upon it as a talisman, instead of giving thanks and praise to Jehovah for their deliverance from bondage.

KING-MAKING BY A STONE

As early as *c.* 1209 BC a stone was used at the crowning of their kings, for we read:

> 'And all the men of Shechem gathered together, and all the house of Millo, and went, and made Abimelech king, by the plain (marginal note, 'oak') of the pillar that was in Shechem' (*Judges* 9: 6).

These words, 'by the oak of the pillar,' show that Abimelech was crowned by the stone which Joshua set up when he gathered all the tribes of Israel together at Shechem, after the land of Canaan had been divided among them; and note, Shechem was where the bones of Joseph were buried. Joshua recited to them all the blessings and guidance which God had given them from the days of Abraham: how He had brought them out of Egypt and over Jordan, and, upbraiding them for forsaking the Lord, called upon them to put away strange gods which were among them, and return to the worship of Jehovah.

> 'And the people said unto Joshua, The Lord our God will we serve, and His voice will we obey. So Joshua made a covenant with the people that day, and set them a statue and an ordinance in Shechem. And Joshua wrote these words in the BOOK OF THE LAW OF GOD, and TOOK A GREAT STONE, and set it up there under AN OAK, that was by THE SANCTUARY of the Lord. And Joshua said unto all the people, Behold, this STONE shall be a WITNESS unto us; FOR IT HATH HEARD ALL THE WORDS OF THE LORD WHICH HE SPAKE UNTO US: it shall be therefore a WITNESS UNTO YOU, LEST YE DENY YOUR GOD' (*Joshua* 24:24-27).

'It (the stone) heard all the words of the Lord which He spake unto us.' What words? And when? And where? Surely, all the words that God had spoken to them 'out of Egypt,' and 'over Jordan,' which Joshua had recapitulated: 'for the Lord our God, He it is that brought us up and our fathers out of the land of Egypt, from the house of bondage, and which did those great signs in our sight.' The stone had been a reminder of the covenant between themselves and God, a witness 'by the Sanctuary of the Lord.'

'... BY A PILLAR AS THE MANNER WAS'

Another coronation worth noting, and one which brings us to the Temple, is that of Joash; an attempt was being made to place a puppet on the throne, but Jehoiada the priest gave orders to the guard:

> 'And the guard stood, every man with his weapons in his hand, round about the king, from the right corner of the temple to the left corner of the temple, along by the altar and the temple. And he brought forth the king's son, and put the crown upon him, and gave him the testimony; and they made him king, and anointed him; and they clapped their hands, and said, God save the King. And when Athaliah [who had attempted to attain power] heard the noise of the guard and of the people, she came to the people into the temple

of the Lord. And when she looked, behold, the king stood by a pillar, as the manner was, and the princes and the trumpeters by the king' (II *Kings* 11:11-14).

And so we have arrived in the Temple with a sacred and symbolic stone or pillar still occupying a mysterious and solemn role in the 'headship' of Israel. A stone by which kings stood, 'as the manner was,' when being crowned.

A WARNING PROPHECY?

From what source the Masonic Craft deduces the belief that our Coronation Stone was a capstone of the Temple, after the builders had failed several times to find a suitable position for it, we must leave them to explain from their secret traditions, but their conviction cannot fail to bring to mind the prophecy of David, 'The stone which the builders refused is become the head stone of the corner. This is the Lord's doing; it is marvellous in our eyes' (*Psalm* 118:22, 23).

This prophecy certainly contains a simile foretelling the rejection of Christ by the Jews, and the purpose of His First Advent as laying the foundation of His Kingdom of which He was to be the Corner Stone; yet, of what value is a simile if it has no counterpart in the actual life or history of the people to whom the simile was given? Otherwise they could not be expected to understand the allusion, and the simile would be useless.

We must remember that the prophecy with its simile was given to the Jews, not to the Gentile Church. The Stone of Israel was a symbol of the promise to Jacob, 'In thee and in thy seed shall all families of the earth be blessed.' This prophecy, although given to Jacob when he had the vision while resting on the Stone, pointed towards their Messiah in Whom all families of the earth would be blessed. If, therefore, they were in due course to be aware that the Stone had been refused by the builders and finally had become a capstone of their Temple, it was a warning prophecy to them that He Whom they would reject was He Who was to be, in spite of them, their Messiah.

It is but fair also to mention the Mohammedan belief that Jacob's Stone was brought to Jerusalem, and is still preserved in the mosque now standing where the Temple once stood. [34]

---

[34] STACPOOLE, op.cit. p. 83.

JEREMIAH IN EGYPT
About the year 598 BC, Jeremiah, by God's instruction, prophesied:

'Behold, I will give this city into the hand of the king of Babylon, and he shall burn it with fire: and thou [Zedekiah the King] shalt not escape out of his hand' (*Jeremiah* 34:2-3).

This prophecy was fulfilled in *c.* 588 BC and, the king's sons having been killed and Zedekiah himself taken prisoner to Babylon, there remained only the king's daughters.

In the *Encyclopaedia Britannica*, under 'Daphnae', the following information is given:

'**Daphnae** (Tahpanhes, mod. *Defenneh*), an ancient fortress near the Syrian frontier of Egypt, on the Pelusian arm of the Nile. Here King Psammetichus established a garrison of foreign mercenaries, mostly Carians and Ionian Greeks. After the destruction of Jerusalem by Nebuchadnezzar in 588 BC, the Jewish fugitives, of whom Jeremiah was one, came to Tahpanhes... The site was discovered by Sir Flinders Petrie in 1886; the name "Castle of the Jew's Daughter" seems to preserve the tradition of the Jewish refugees.' [35]

THE HOUSE OF DAVID IN SPAIN
We know that Jeremiah went to Egypt with the king's daughters, and, although the Masonic tradition does not mention Spain, we find exceedingly interesting information in Dr. Isaac da Costa's *Israel and the Gentiles*:

'Without enlarging upon the hypothesis that King Solomon possessed both colonies and jurisdiction in Spain (supposed to be the Tarshish of Scripture), tradition on every side agrees in fixing the establishment of Jews in this country at a date soon after the destruction of the first Temple. This tradition... informs us, that... many families of the tribe of Judah, and of the House of David, established themselves in this country, and built cities,

---

[35] *Encyclopaedia Britannica* 14th edition. 1946. Vol. 7, p.48.

the names of which still recall localities and reminiscences of Palestine'.

Dr. da Costa also states:

'As a nation within a nation the Sephardic Jews are especially remarkable for the early date of their settlement in the Peninsula (Spanish). The time of the first settlement was formerly reckoned by both Jewish and Christian authors as belonging to the periods of the Babylonian exile.' [36]

JEREMIAH'S TOMB IN IRELAND?

It was Jeremiah who warned King Zedekiah of the coming destruction of Jerusalem. If the Stone was either in the Temple or part of the Temple building it is hardly likely that the prophet would leave such a precious relic to be amongst the ruins and thus destroyed or lost. It is but reasonable to suppose that he carried it with him to Egypt, but, whether it was Simon Breck from Spain, or Jeremiah from Egypt who took the Stone to Ireland, there is a link in Ireland with Jeremiah: there is a tradition that suggests that a tomb hewn out of rock in a cemetery on Devenish Island, in Lough Erne, is known as 'Jeremiah's Tomb.' [37]

Let us leave Ireland by quoting Sir William Bentham, Ulster King-of-Arms, on the ancient language of its people, in his *Etruria-Celtica*:

'Ireland, situated in the Western extremity of Europe and separated by a tempestuous sea, escaping, by that circumstance, Roman conquest and colonisation, was the only spot in Europe where the ancient Celtic language continued to be spoken in purity.'
'The Truscan (language) is, in fact, the simple uncompounded Celtic or Phoenician, and the Celts were Phoenician colonies.'
'Sanctes Marmocchinus in his *MS* essay in defence of the Etruscan language, and Sigismund Titius in his History of Etruria, think that the Etruscan was mixed up with Hebrew... Baldus considers it Chaldean and Hebrew. Jacobus Mantinus, a Jew, and Theseus Ambrosius, consider it Assyrian and Hebrew.' [38]

---

[36] DA COSTA op.cit. p. 211; p. 157.
[37] Research carried out at Cairn T, Loughcrew in Co. Meath, it has been suggested, could indicate that Jeremiah was buried here. See CONWELL, E., *Ollamh Fodhla*. Bishop Auckland: Covenant Publishing Company Ltd, 2005.
[38] BENTHAM, op.cit. p. 4; p. 44; p. 46.

Thus the language and the people of the Stone seem certainly to have passed to Ireland.

(XI)   It was removed to Scotland

We are told by Canon Murray in his book *The King's Crowning*: 'After old Scots custom on the Coronation of Charles II at Scone in 1651, Lyon King-of-Arms rehearsed the royal line of Kings from the days of Fergus I, 330 BC.' [39]

This Fergus, King of Ireland, invaded Scotland, and we read in George Buchanan's *History of Scotland*: 'Fergus returning home victorious (to Ireland) the Scots confirmed the kingdom to him and his posterity by an oath.' [40]

Dr. Geoffrey Keating, in his *Forus Feasa ar Eirinn*, tells us:

'... It is it (the Stone) that is called "Lia Fail"; and it is it that used to roar under each king of Ireland on his being chosen by them... and it is that stone called in Latin "*Saxum Fatale.*"

'This stone which is called "Lia Fail," another name for it is the Stone of Destiny; for it was in destiny for this stone whatever place it would be in, that it is a man of the Scotic nation, i.e. of the seed of Mileadh of Spain, that would be in the sovereignty of that country, according as is read in Hector Boetius in the *History of Scotland*...

'When the race of Scots heard that the stone had this virtue, after Feargus the great, son of Earc, had obtained power of Scotland, and after he had proposed to style himself King of Scotland, he sends information into the presence of his brother Muircheartach, son of Earc, of the race of Eireamhon, who was the king of Ireland at that time, to ask him to send him this stone, to sit upon, for the purpose of being proclaimed King of Scotland. Muircheartach sends the stone to him, and he was the first King of Scotland of the Scottish nation.' [41]

Of Kenneth II, George Buchanan's *History of Scotland* says:

[39] MURRAY, CANON ROBERT HENRY. *The King's Crowning*. London: John Murray, 1937. p. 141.
[40] BUCHANAN, op.cit. Vol. i, book. iv. p.158.
[41] KEATING, op.cit. Vol. i, p. 207.

'The marble block which Simon Breccus is said to have imported from Spain to Ireland, and Fergus, son of Ferchard, carried thence to Argyle in Scottish Albium, he caused to be removed from Argyle to Scoon on the river Tay, and set it there enclosed in a chair of wood. In that seat the kings of Scotland used to receive the title and insignia of Royalty until the time of Edward I of England.' [42]

The Fergus referred to in this paragraph is Fergus II, who died AD 501, and the 'marble block' was the Stone.

The earliest reference to the Stone by a Scottish writer is in 1301, by Baldred Bisset in his *Processus Baldredi contra figmenta Regis Angliæ*, which, it should be noted, is only about five years after Edward I carried the relic to England. His historical remarks are so condensed that they only add confusion to the chronological problem; they are:

'The daughter of Pharaoh, King of Egypt, with an armed band and a large fleet, goes to Ireland, and there being joined by a body of Irish, she sails to Scotland, taking with her the royal seat which he, the King of England, with other insignia of the Kingdom of Scotland, carried with him by violence to England. She conquered and destroyed the Picts and took their Kingdom, and from this Scota the Scots and Scotia are named.' [43]

ST. COLUMBA AND THE STONE

Before the Stone was transferred by Kenneth II from Dunstaffnage to Scone in AD 846, Columba, one of the early Christian missionaries to Scotland, had made Iona his principal seat. He was born in Donegal on December 7, 521, and was the son of Feidlimid who was a member of the Royal House of Ireland. Iona in Gaelic is known as 'Innis nan Druidhneah' or 'Island of Druids.'

'According to Bede, Iona was given by the Picts to Columba about 550. According to the Annals of Ulster, and of Tighernac, which Archbishop Ussher seems disposed to follow, the Island of

[42] BUCHANAN, op.cit. Vol.i. book. vi. p. 275.
[43] BISSET, BALDRED (rector of Kinghorn) *Processus Baldredi contra figmenta Regis Angliæ 1301*, to the Papal Curia of 1301 against the claims of the English King, Edward I, ref. in SKENE, W. F., op.cit. p. 19.

Iona was given to Columba by Conal, or Conval, the son of Congal, king of the Dalriad Scots.' [44]

And Dean Stanley, in his *Historical Memorials of Westminster Abbey*, mentions the legend that, when dying, Columba asked to be carried to 'the Stone that he might finish his life's work with his head resting on it.'[45] Other records, however, state that he died before the altar in the Abbey.

'According to Adamnan,' in *Life of St. Columba*, 'he had the bare rock for pallet and a stone for pillow, which to this day stands by his grave as his monumental pillar.' [46]

It is this fact which has caused the confused idea that this stone which he used as a pillow, and which is still in Iona Abbey, is the Stone of Destiny, namely 'Lia Fail' or 'Jacob's Pillar,' in spite of the fact that according to tradition the Stone of Destiny was transferred to Dunstaffnage:

'On this stone – the old Druidic Stone of Destiny, sacred among the Gael before Christ was born – Columba crowned Aidan, King of Argyll. Later the stone was taken to Dunstaffnage, where the Lords of the Isles were made princes: thence to Scone, where the last Celtic Kings of Scotland were crowned on it.' [47]

Canon Murray, in his *The King's Crowning*, states:

'The most ancient coronation rite in Europe is our own, for it stretched back to the days of the inauguration of Aidan by Columba in the seventh century.'
'The earliest known description of the consecration of a king, Aidan by name (d. AD 605), in Great Britain occurs in the *Life of St. Columba* written by St. Adamnan, who was Abbot of Iona. In this seventh-century description the term *ordinare regem*, the ordination of the King, occurs, and the laying-on of hands by the Abbot on the King's head is plainly indicated. The decisive words are, "During the words of consecration the saint (Columba)

[44] BUCHANAN, op.cit. Vol.i, book.i, p. 45 (notes).
[45] STANLEY, op.cit 4th edition, p. 47.
[46] MCNEILL, F. MARIAN ed. *An Iona Anthology.* Iona Community, 1990. p. 22.
[47] MACLEOD, FIONA (William Sharp). *Iona.* London, 1910. p. 67.

declared the future regarding the *children, grandchildren*, and *great-grandchildren* of Aidan, and, laying his hand upon his head, he consecrated and blessed him". ' [48]

(The italics are the author's to emphasize that this declaring of the future generations of Aidan was exactly what was done by Jacob when he blessed his sons before he died.)

Columba seems to have had the gift of prophecy, for, apart from declaring the future of Aidan's posterity, he is said to have foretold:

'In Iona of my heart, Iona of my love,
Instead of monks' voices shall be lowing of cattle,
But ere the world come to an end
Iona shall be as it was.'

The Abbey of Iona eventually fell into complete ruin, and, as he foretold, cattle grazed within and around its walls; but in 1899 the 8th Duke of Argyll gifted the Abbey to the Church of Scotland. The restoration of the whole Abbey was commenced in 1938 by 'The Iona Community', under the leadership of the Rev. Dr. George MacLeod, and was completed in 1965. [49]

A further piece of evidence that the Scottish kings originally came from Ireland is given in Buchanan's *History of Scotland*:

'In the Abbey of Saint Columba, the bishops of the Isles fixed their residence, after their ancient seat in Eubonia was taken possession of by the English. Amidst the ruins there remains still a burying place, or cemetery, common to all the noble families of the Western Islands, in which, conspicuous above the rest, stand three tombs, at a little distance from each other; on these are placed three sacred shrines turned towards the East, and on their Western sides are fixed small tablets, with the inscriptions indicating to whom the tombs belong. That which is in the middle, has as its title, TUMULUS REGUM SCOTIAE, the Tomb of the Kings of Scotland, for there forty-eight kings of the Scots are said to have been buried. The one upon the right is inscribed, TUMULUS REGUM HIBERNIAE, the Tomb of the Kings of Ireland,

---

[48] MURRAY, op.cit. p.107; p. 45.
[49] The Abbey restoration was completed in 1965, from which time The Iona Community has run it as a residential centre, and daily worship has continued in the Abbey Church.

where four Irish kings are reported to rest. And upon the one upon the left is engraved, TUMULUS REGUM NORVEGIAE, the Tomb of the Kings of Norway, general rumour having assigned to it the ashes of eight Norwegian kings.' [50]

In comparison with the records which have already been quoted, the last crowning of a king of the Scots over the Stone, that of John Baliol, is recent history, for, immediately after, in 1296, Edward I of England captured it, and took it back with him to England where he placed it in Westminster Abbey.

SCOTTISH CORONATIONS

In due course the crowns of Scotland and England were united in the person of James VI of Scotland, who became James I of Britain, and it is interesting to know something of the form of the coronation service of these ancient Scottish kings. The Marquess of Bute, in his book *Scottish Coronations*, tells us that seven prayers were used at the ancient coronation of the Scots Kings. The following are extracts.

Prayer IV
'Lord, who from everlasting governest the kingdom of all kings, bless thou this ruling prince. Amen.'
'And glorify him with such blessing that he may hold the sceptre of Salvation in the exaltation of David, and be found rich with the gifts of sanctifying mercy. Amen.'
'Grant unto him by thine inspiration even to rule the people in meekness as thou didst cause Solomon to obtain a kingdom of peace. Amen.'
Prayer V
'Almighty God give thee the dew of heaven and the fatness of the earth, and plenty of corn and wine. Let people serve thee and nations bow down to thee; be lord over thy brethren and let thy mother's sons bow down to thee. God shall be thine helper, and the Almighty shall bless thee with blessings of heaven above, on the mountains and on the hills, blessings of the deep that lieth under, blessings of the breasts and of grapes and apples. The blessings of the ancient fathers, Abraham, and Isaac, and Jacob, be confirmed upon thee. Amen.'

---

[50] BUCHANAN, op.cit. Vol. i, book. i, p. 46.

Prayer VI

'Bless, O Lord, the substance of our prince, and accept the work of his hands; and blessed of thee be his hand, for the precious things of heaven, for the dew, and for the deep that coucheth beneath, and for the precious fruits brought forth by the sun, and for the precious things put forth by the moon, and for the chief things of the ancient mountains, and for the precious things of the lasting hills, and fulness thereof; the blessing of Him that appeared in the bush come upon the head of (name); and let the blessing of the Lord be full upon his children; and let him dip his feet in oil, let his horns be like the horns of unicorns, with them he shall push the people together to the end of the earth, for let Him who rideth upon the heaven be his help for ever. Amen.' [51]

The Marquess of Bute also quotes from a pamphlet entitled, *The Forme and Order of the Coronation of Charles the Second, King of Scotland, England, France and Ireland. As it was acted and done at Scone, the first day of January, 1651.* It is the work of Sir James Balfour, the Lord Lyon King-of Arms, who officiated upon the occasion. The minister, who gave the sermon and exhortations from which the following extracts are taken, was the Rev. Robert Dowglas.

'When the King was set down upon the throne, the Minister spoke to him a word of exhortation:
' "Sir, you are set down upon the throne in a very difficult time; I shall therefore put you in mind of a Scriptural expression of a Throne; it is said: 'Solomon sate on the Throne of the Lord.' Sir, you are a king, and a king in covenant with the Lord."
' "It is the Lord's Throne. Remember that you have a King above you, the King of Kings, and Lord of Lords, who commandeth thrones."
' "Your Throne is the Lord's Throne, and your people are the Lord's people. Let not your heart be lifted up above your brethren (*Deuteronomy* 17:20). They are your brethren, not only flesh of your flesh, but brethren by covenant with God."
' "Your Throne is the Lord's Throne. Beware of making His Throne a Throne of iniquity."

---

[51] JOHN, THIRD MARQUESS OF BUTE, *Scottish Coronations*. Paisley and London, 1902. pp. 49-58.

' "But as the Throne is the Lord's Throne, let the laws be the Lord's laws, agreeable to His Word."

' "Lastly, if your Throne be the Throne of the Lord, take a word of encouragement against thine adversaries. Your enemies are the enemies of the Lord's Throne." ' [52]

THE SCOTTISH DECLARATION OF INDEPENDENCE

Before leaving Scotland to record the last resting place of this strange relic, another incident requires to be considered.

King Robert the Bruce, the next Scottish king after the removal of the Stone to Westminster, was visited by two emissaries of Pope John XXII, to whom Edward II of England had appealed for help to compel Scotland to acknowledge England's lordship. These emissaries bore a message from the Pope advising Bruce to submit to Edward's claims, but Bruce and his nobles drafted a letter which they addressed to Pope John XXII and which can still be seen in the Register House in Edinburgh. It has attached to it coloured ribbons and seals with the signatures of Robert the Bruce and twenty-five of his nobles. The letter, which was dated April 6, 1320, reads:

'We know Most Holy Father and Lord, and from the chronicles and books of the ancients gather, that among other illustrious nations, ours, to wit, the nation of the Scots, has been distinguished by many honours; which, passing from the greater Scythia through the Mediterranean Sea and Pillars of Hercules and sojourning in Spain among the most savage tribes through a long course of time, could nowhere be subjugated by any people however barbarous; and coming thence one thousand two hundred years after the outgoing of the People of Israel, they, by many victories and infinite toil, acquired for themselves the possessions in the West which they now hold... In their kingdom one hundred and thirteen kings of their own royal stock, no stranger intervening, have reigned...'

This letter gathers into one record the main points of the various traditions: that the people who had the Stone were connected with the

[52] ibid. pp.141, 142, ref. from BALFOUR, SIR JAMES *The Forme and Order of the Coronation of Charles the Second, King of Scotland, England, France and Ireland. As it was acted and done at Scone, the first day of January, 1651* pp.191-201.

ancient people of Israel; that they came from the Middle East; that they passed through the Mediterranean, dwelt in Spain for a period, and eventually came over to these Islands; and that their royal line of kings has remained unbroken throughout their migrations.

Those who wish to discount the value of the statements made in this letter bring forward the claim that Irish records abound with chronological references to Israel, and so they seem to be merely a method of recording the period of world history in which certain Irish events took place; but as the Israelites had not even been a nation since 588 BC, why should any people unconnected with them wish continually to measure their history by events in Israel's records? The very fact that chronological references to Israel abound in Irish records is circumstantial evidence for some connection with them.

Research findings have indicated that Irish monkish editors have tampered with these ancient legends and given a fantastic chronology to the events, making the departure of the 'Lia Fail' and Scota an event of the time of Moses. The account preserved by the Welsh historian Nennius (*fl.* 796)[53] does not seem to have suffered in monkish hands, and according to his chronology this arrival in Ireland occurred 1,002 years after the Exodus, namely *c.* 484 BC, within a century of the removal of Jeremiah and the only surviving heirs of the House of David, the King's 'daughters' (*Jeremiah* 43:6), to Tahpanhes in Egypt.

A SCEPTIC REFUTED

In an article in the Scottish *Daily Mail* (26.12.50), on the day after the theft, Lewis Spence states:

> 'A general notion prevails that it is of Irish origin, and that it is actually the "Lia Fail", or Stone of Destiny, spoken of in Irish tradition which was brought to Scotland by conquering Irish Scots from the Hill of Tara. Frankly there are no grounds for assuming the credibility of this time-honoured notion.'

The reader must decide for himself what importance to place on such a sweeping statement in the light of the records and traditions already quoted.

---

[53] NENNIUS, *Historia Brittonum (History of the Britons)*. Trans. Giles, J.A. London: George Bell and Sons, 1891.

Mr. Spence continues: 'The Coronation Stone, as we know it, can most definitely be proved to have been situated in the Royal Scottish demesne at Scone in the thirteenth century until it was removed to Westminster by Edward I in the year 1296.' [54] Certainly, but for how many years previous to 1296 was it at Scone? According to tradition this was from the time Kenneth II removed it to Scone from Dunstaffnage in 846.

Surely, if the Stone was originally quarried near Scone for the purpose of the King's Seat, there would be some record, either written or handed down as tradition, of such an important innovation; but no such record or tradition has been found of a local stone being either made or used for the first time as the King's Seat.

Again, if the Stone was just a stone quarried locally to fulfil the old custom of their ancestors of having the King seated on a stone at his coronation, then, why, when it was stolen by Edward I, was not another stone immediately and similarly quarried at Scone, and the custom continued during the intervening 300 years from the crowning of Robert the Bruce to that of James VI? Surely because, to only one Stone, the Stone of Destiny, was attached the traditions necessary as a family, or national, heirloom.

Mr. Spence adds: 'Most Scottish folk once devoutly believed that the Stone at Scone was that which had been carried from Ireland to Argyll and thence to Scone. But Irish antiquaries have proved conclusively that the real Lia Fail of the ancient Hibernian Kings, which was erected on the hill of Tara, is still there.' It is strange that, in spite of these 'conclusive proofs' which are of the same standard of conclusiveness as all the other evidence concerning the early history of the Stone, this Tara 'Lia Fail' should have passed into oblivion to all save antiquarians, while the so-called spurious stone has remained in great prominence and of national importance right to the present time.

But there are more doubtful points to consider. This stone which is still at Tara is, according to *The Coronation Regalia*, [55] of a rough cylindrical shape, rounded at the top, and, while standing six feet above the ground, is sunk six feet into the ground, namely twelve feet high. It is said to have been brought to Ireland by the Tuatha de Danaans from Northern Europe, not by the people of Scota from Spain.

The most suggestive evidence, however, for the Scottish Stone being the original Jacob's Stone, apart from the traditions attached to it, is the

---

[54] SPENCE, LEWIS, taken from his book *Magic Arts in Celtic Britain*. London: Rider & Co., 1945. p. 99.
[55] STACPOOLE, op.cit. pp. 85, 86.

fact that the Coronation Stone is in the natural shape and size of a pillow, namely 26 in. by 16 in. by 10 ½ in., while a cylindrical stone such as the one at Tara could hardly be called suitable. Furthermore, the Bible states that Jacob poured oil upon the top of the Stone, and this would not have been possible if the Stone had been twelve feet high as is the one at Tara. And what of the weight? The small Coronation Stone weighs over three hundredweight, the weight of the Tara Stone must be over a ton, not a relic suitable for long migrations as the traditions claim.

Although the Stone is not mentioned in records of Scots coronations of early periods, it is likewise only rarely mentioned in coronation records all down the centuries till even the present time.

(XII)   It was taken to Westminster Abbey

On a postcard illustration of the Coronation Chair and the Stone, formerly sold at the bookstall in Westminster Abbey, there is a description of them by Lawrence Turner, M.V.O., F.S.A., Keeper of the Muniments of the Abbey, which contains these statements:

> 'The Chair was made in 1300 to enclose the Stone of Scone... This famous Stone has a legendary history which identifies it with Jacob's pillow at Bethel, the Lia Fail (Stone of Destiny) of Tara, and the Chair of St. Columba at Iona... It has been used in the Abbey at every Coronation from Edward II's to that of his present Majesty.'

It has already been recorded that Edward I confiscated it and made it the crowning stone of England and of his successors; and we have noted that James VI of Scotland eventually became King of England by the same rightful succession, thus following the Stone. Now we must record two strangely interesting episodes which show how the minds of both the authorities in power, and even the 'common people' regarded the traditions of their monarchy, and the importance of the Stone.

James VI and I, when coming to take over the throne of England (1603), thus uniting the two Kingdoms, entered the City of London through Aldersgate, or Gate of the Elders, which was taken down in 1761, and which was one of the gates of the ancient City.

This gate had over its centre arch, on the north side, figures of the prophets Samuel and Jeremiah, with inscriptions below the figures:

Under Samuel: 'And Samuel said unto all Israel, Behold, I have hearkened unto your voice in all that ye said unto me, and have made a king over you.'

Under Jeremiah: 'Then shall there enter into the gates of this city kings and princes sitting upon the throne of David, riding in chariots and on horses, they, and their princes, the men of Judah, and the inhabitants of Jerusalem: and this city shall remain for ever.'

A small representation in metal of the gate used to be fixed on the railings of the churchyard of St. Botolph's Church in Little Britain, off Aldersgate Street. The visitor might well ask what connection have Samuel, Jeremiah and David of Israel with the entry of a British King to his capital for crowning? Why should those responsible erect these figures, and use these words on such an occasion?

WHY A TREATY WAS BROKEN

Dean Stanley, in his *Historical Memorials of Westminster Abbey*, when dealing with the Stone, quotes Ayloffe's *Calendar of Ancient Charters* (p. 58), which states:

'A solemn article in the Treaty of Northampton which closed the long war between the two countries required the restoration of the lost relic to Scotland. Accordingly, Edward III, then residing at Bardesly, directed his writ under Privy Seal to the Abbot and Convent of Westminster commanding them to give the Stone for this purpose to the Sheriffs of London who would receive the same by indenture, and cause it to be carried to the Queen-mother. All the other articles of the treaty were fulfilled, even "the Black Rood", the sacred cross of the Holy Rood, which Edward I had carried off with the other relics, was restored. But, "the Stone of Scone", on which the Kings of Scotland used at Scone to be placed, on their inauguration, the people of London would by no means whatever allow to depart from themselves.' [56]

---

[56] STANLEY, op.cit. 4th edn. pp. 59-60. ref. Ayloffe, Sir Joseph, sixth baronet (1709/10–1781), antiquary. He held the office of Keeper of the State Paper Office in 1763. He edited *Calendars of the Ancient Charters, etc. and of the Welsh and Scottish Rolls in the Tower of London*, published 1772.

In the *Chronicon de Lanercost* [57] we are told that the Regalia was taken from the Tower of London without any protest by the people, but when the Commissioners sought to remove the Stone from Westminster Abbey 'the people of London would in no wise allow to be taken away from them the Stone of Scone, whereon the Kings of Scotland used to be set at their Coronation at Scone.'

It is events such as these that caused Disraeli to say, 'A tradition can neither be made nor destroyed,' and is not Sir Arnold Wilson equally right in saying, 'Tradition is a sort of accumulated commonsense of centuries, a sort of balance to keep us on an even keel'?

THE THEFT AND THE PETITION

There are occasions, however, when a lack of knowledge of a tradition leads to acts that are not in keeping with the mantle of dignity that millenniums of time have cast over a relic. Such an occasion occurred on Christmas Day, 1950. Early in the morning of that day it was discovered that Westminster Abbey had been broken into by thieves who had stolen the Coronation Stone from under King Edward's Chair, badly damaging the Chair, and had dragged the Stone from the Abbey, thus committing acts of common theft and sacrilege.

A week after the theft a letter was handed into the office of a Glasgow newspaper, the *Daily Record*, asking that one copy of the Petition accompanying it should go to the Police and the other to the Press. The Petition, which by its phraseology was obviously drafted by someone familiar with the law, stated:

'The petition of certain of his Majesty's most loyal and obedient subjects to his Majesty, King George the Sixth humbly sheweth: That his Majesty's petitioners are the persons who removed the Stone of Destiny from Westminster Abbey.

'That, in removing the Stone of Destiny, they have no desire to injure his Majesty's property, nor to pay disrespect to the Church of which he is the temporal head.

'That the Stone of Destiny is, however, the most ancient symbol of Scottish nationality and, having been removed from Scotland by force and retained in England in breach of the pledge of his Majesty's predecessor King Edward III of England and its proper

---

[57] STEVENSON. J. ed. *Chronicon de Lanercost 1201-1346*. Edinburgh, 1839. p. 261.

place of retention is among his Majesty's Scottish people who, above all, hold this symbol dear.

'That therefore his Majesty's petitioners will most readily return the Stone to the safe keeping of his Majesty's officers if his Majesty will but graciously assure them that in all time coming the Stone will remain in Scotland in such of his Majesty's properties or otherwise as shall be deemed fitting by him.

'That such an assurance will in no way preclude the use of the Stone in any coronation of any of his Majesty's successors whether in England or Scotland.

'That his Majesty's humble petitioners are prepared to submit to his Majesty's Ministers or their representatives proof that they are the people able, willing, and eager to restore the Stone of Destiny to the keeping of his Majesty's officers.

'That his Majesty's petitioners, who have served him in peril and peace, pledge again their loyalty to him, saving always their right and duty to protest against the actions of his Ministers if such actions are contrary to the wishes of the spirit of his Majesty's Scottish people.

'In witness of the good faith of his Majesty's petitioners the following information concerning a watch left in Westminster Abbey on December 25, 1950, is appended: (1) The mainspring of the watch was recently repaired; (2) The bar holding the right-hand wrist strap to the watch had recently been broken and soldered.

'This information is given in lieu of signature by his Majesty's petitioners, being in fear of apprehension.' [58]

Of their loyalty there may be no doubt, but 'misguided subjects' would have been a more fitting term than 'obedient', since on their own admission they have flagrantly disobeyed his Majesty's laws by committing theft and sacrilege, and have also, in effect, and with however humble words, blackmailed the King by offering terms for the safe return of the Stone without disclosing their identity, 'being in fear of apprehension.'

The author, and most if not all of his Scottish compatriots, would like Scotland to have the handling of her domestic affairs by her own

---

[58] *The Scotsman*, 30th December 1950, p. 5.

Legislature, [59] but he is certain that the majority of them will pray that people like the misguided petitioners will have no part in its deliberation until they have shown public repentance for the shadow which they have so foolishly cast on Scotland's honour and dignity.

Let us examine their Petition in the light of the record of the Stone already given.

(1) They claim it is 'the most ancient symbol of Scottish nationality' and 'its proper place of retention is among his Majesty's Scottish people who, above all, hold this symbol dear.' Why, if this claim to ancient use and sentiment is to be heeded should not the Stone be sent to Ireland for 'retention'? Its traditional connection with Ireland goes back to the BC years. Indeed, in 1884 elaborate plans were made to remove the Stone to Ireland in realisation of the hopes of extreme nationalists there. The unsuccessful attempts by the 'Dynamite Men', as they were called, are described in *Twenty-five Years in the Secret Service* by Major Le Caron:

> 'Its restoration to the land of its original and only lawful owners, it was contended, would inspire confidence in the course then being pursued, and the people would be strengthened by the well-known tradition "that so long as the Stone remained in Ireland, so long would she remain a united nation", while its loss to the English would work wonders. Elaborate preparations were made for carrying out the scheme. Men were sent from America to work in conjunction with certain Fenians in London, and it was decided that some of the conspirators should secrete themselves in the Abbey, and at night seize the police, remove the Stone, and pass it out through a window to others who would be waiting outside to take it to a place of safety. For months these men waited and waited, but the opportunity never came, for one of the group gave the whole thing away to the police, and the detectives who surrounded the sacred edifice made the seizure impossible.' [60]

---

[59] Following a referendum in 1997 in which the Scottish people gave their consent, the current Scottish Parliament was established by the Scotland Act 1998, which sets out its powers as a devolved legislature. The first meeting of the new Parliament took place on May 12, 1999.
[60] LE CARON, MAJOR HENRI. *Twenty Five Years in the Secret Service. The Recollections of a Spy.* 2nd ed. London: William Heinemann Ltd., 1892. p. 244.

(2) They refer to it 'having been removed from Scotland by force'; certainly, Edward I, who was unable to conquer Scotland by force of arms, did what to him seemed the next best thing, he secured the crowning seat of its kings, and took it back to his capital – London. To keep it as a trophy of war is understandable, but to place it in his most sacred shrine, and to have made for it a special Coronation Chair so that his successors could be legally crowned over it, requires a deeper explanation than one of pride of conquest.

In his work, *The Royal House of Britain an Enduring Dynasty,* the late Rev. W. M. H. Milner, M.A., states that, in response to an enquiry which he sent to the Herald's College, he received a letter (dated 5.2.1901) stating that 'There is a very valuable *MS* here, deducing our Saxon Kings from Adam and through David.' Milner continues:

'This *MS* we have inspected. It is called on the back of the binding: "Pedigree of the Saxon Kings." Odin is there, and David is there, but one in one line apparently, and the other in another, unconnected, unless the notes, written in a very difficult script, indicate such connections. We were, however, assured that the impression in the Herald's College had always been that the *MS* traced the Saxon line through David.' [61]

Is it likely that Edward I was ignorant of this tradition, or of the one attached to the Stone of his northern neighbours, any more than the Kaiser, in the present century, was ignorant of the same traditions concerning the Stone? Why was the Stone so carefully hidden during the last two wars? If Edward believed the traditions of the Stone and also that of his own descent from King David, he would feel he had a right to rule over these northern people, and what wish would be more natural than that he should possess the Stone for the crowning of his successors.

(3) They assert that it was 'retained in England in breach of the pledge of his Majesty's predecessor King Edward III of England.' This is correct for, although, according to historical accounts, the reason for retention was the demonstration by the mob against the Stone's removal, that is more of the nature of an excuse than a reason.

But why stop there? Providence has a strange way of making fools of us over our attempts to rectify, as we may think, the working out of

---

[61] MILNER, W. M. H. *The Royal House of Britain an Enduring Dynasty.* 11th ed. London: Covenant Publishing Company Ltd., 1940. p. 23.

history. In 1296 the Stone, which, apart from the strange and fateful traditions attached to it, was merely a symbol of a royal throne, was stolen; in 1603 the English, the people of the country whose king had stolen the Stone, had accepted, because of his legal right, the king of the injured country to rule over them, namely King James VI of Scotland. Could retribution be more complete? Could recompense be more full? Is it possible, even now, to secure a more honourable and satisfying annulment of an injury? The people of England might well have cried, 'We stole your Stone, but now we accept your King'. One might say that Edward I did not so much take a Stone into his capital as a Trojan Horse; for, remember, the legend concerning the Stone ran, 'If fates go right, where'er this Stone is found, the Scots shall monarchs of that realm be found.'

These petitioners are only three centuries too late; Scotland has extended its Royal domain, and taken over new properties for keeping its heirlooms.

It is but fair, however, to apportion blame where it is due, and the extreme nationalistic attitude of so many Scotsmen, and the feeling of separateness from England which should not exist, is caused by the thoughtless and careless use of the term 'England' by so many of those whose high place in national affairs should have taught them to be more judicious, nay, more correct in their speech, for small slips can have grievous effects.

The expressions 'King of England,' 'English Throne,' and 'English Parliament' are so completely wrong that the use of them is a slight to the intelligence of the user as much as to the pride of the other citizens of the Commonwealth, and shows a subtle nationalistic spirit which, in others, they deplore but help to create.

There is no 'King or Queen of England'; the name England is not used in the Coronation Service; the wording is unmistakably clear. It is: 'Will you solemnly promise and swear to govern the peoples of Great Britain, Ireland, Canada, Australia, New Zealand and the Union of South Africa... according to their respective laws and customs?' Let us hope that in future those who occupy high places will show an example to others in being careful not to give offence, and in being correct in their use of important national terms.

(4) They undertake to return the Stone 'if his Majesty will but graciously assure them that in all time coming, the Stone will remain in

Scotland.' As the legend has once worked out to the full, the petitioners should bear in mind that it may do so again, and so, if they have their wish, in future the Scots would be monarchs of their own tiny kingdom only, instead of monarchs of not only Great Britain, but of the greatest Commonwealth of Free and Equal Nations the world has ever known.

The first Scottish King who would have been crowned over the Stone, had it not been stolen by Edward I, was Robert the Bruce. To-day we have a Monarch who is descended from that famous Scottish King,[62] a fact which makes the condition that the Stone should remain in Scotland doubly absurd and the Stone a doubly personal heirloom to the Crown, as well as a national heirloom to all the people over whom the Monarch rules.

In the process of removing the Stone from Westminster Abbey, it had been broken in two and subsequently mended by a stonemason in Scotland. It was left in Arbroath Abbey on April 11, 1951, four months after it had been taken. The four students involved did not face prosecution. [63]

During the twentieth century there were four coronations with the Stone as the crowning seat, and some readers will at least remember the crowning of the present Monarch.

THE VEIL OF THE ETERNAL

Canon Murray of Worcester, in his book *The King's Crowning*, paints a complete picture of what the Coronation Ceremony means, and what it borrows from the ancient past, and from the mysterious spiritual 'presence' which he calls the 'veil of the eternal.' Let us consider his words:

> 'At the earliest Anglo-Saxon coronations a horn was used, as when Samuel anointed Saul.'
> 'No other ceremony can vie with our coronation in dignity or antiquity.'
> 'To many the coronation is a thrilling pageant, yet to the thoughtful it is much more. To them it is the service that testifies

---

[62] See appendix for genealogical chart: the descent of her Majesty Queen Elizabeth II from Robert I King of Scotland.
[63] The students were all members of a pro-independence group, the Scottish Covenant Association - Ian Hamilton, a law student, Gavin Vernon and Alan Stuart, engineering students, and Kay Matheson, a domestic science student. Ian Hamilton has written his own book on the events of the time (pub: Birlinn Ltd: 2008).

emphatically to the double character of the sovereign, for this service shares a priestly as well as a military character, and to anyone who peruses it carefully it is obvious that the priestly character predominates in it.'

'The coronation is not only the renewal of a time-honoured rite, the celebration of the hallowing of our sovereign – it is all this and much more besides… it is becoming increasingly evident that the Crown has become the symbol of the destiny of the British race, the outward and visible sign of its unity.'

'In the Abbey we can – if we will – see the veil of the eternal through the temporal.' [64]

THE CORONATION CEREMONY AND THE HOUSE OF DAVID

Let the record of the Stone end with a summary of the Coronation Ceremony of which it is such an integral symbol, a ceremony which one could believe had been built round the tradition of the Stone and its mysterious past.

From *The Form and Order of Service for the Coronation of Her Majesty Queen Elizabeth II, 2nd June 1953* we learn that there are fifteen Acts in the Coronation Service:

(i)   *The Preparation*, which commences with the Litany and contains the prayer: 'O God we have heard with our ears, and OUR FATHERS have declared unto us, the noble works that thou didst IN THEIR DAYS, and in the OLD TIME before them,' sung before the arrival of the Queen.

(ii) *The Entrance into the Church*, during which is sung the Anthem: 'I was glad,' which is from *Psalm* 122: 'Our feet shall stand in thy gates O JERUSALEM. JERUSALEM is built as a city that is at unity in itself. O pray for the peace of Jerusalem.'

(iii) *The Recognition*, in which the Queen stands up and shows herself to all the people assembled while the Archbishop says: 'Sirs, I here present unto you Queen Elizabeth, your undoubted Queen: Wherefore all you who are come this day to do your homage and service, Are you willing to do the same? The People then signify their willingness and joy, by

---

[64] MURRAY, op.cit. p. 85; p. 42; p. 44; p. 130; p. 131.

loud and repeated acclamations, all with one voice crying out: 'GOD SAVE QUEEN ELIZABETH.'

Concerning the crowning of Israel's first King, Saul, we read: 'And when Samuel had caused all the tribes of Israel to come near... Samuel said to all the people, SEE YE HIM whom the Lord hath chosen, that there is none like him among all the people? And all the people shouted, and said, GOD SAVE THE KING' (I *Samuel* 10:20-24).

(iv) *The Oath.*

(v) *The Presenting of the Holy Bible* by the Archbishop, who shall first say these words: 'Our gracious Queen; we present you with this Book, the most valuable thing that this world affords. Here is wisdom; THIS IS THE ROYAL LAW; these are the lively Oracles of God.'

(vi) *The Beginning of the Communion Service.*

(vii) *The Anointing.* The account of Samuel anointing Saul is: 'Then Samuel took a vial of oil, and poured it upon his head... and said, Is it not because the Lord hath anointed thee to be captain over His inheritance?' (I *Samuel* 10:1).

The instructions for our present ceremony are: The choir shall sing: 'ZADOK the PRIEST and NATHAN the PROPHET anointed SOLOMON King; and all the people rejoiced and said: GOD SAVE THE KING, Long live the King, May the King live for ever. Amen, Hallelujah' (I *Kings* 1:39, 40).

The Queen shall sit down in King Edward's Chair... to be anointed (this is the Chair under the seat of which rests 'the Stone').

The Archbishop shall anoint the Queen in the form of a cross:

1. On the palms of both hands, saying: 'Be thy Hands anointed with holy Oil.'

2. On the breast, saying: 'Be thy Breast anointed with holy Oil.'

3. On the crown of the head, saying: 'Be thy HEAD anointed with holy Oil, as KINGS, PRIESTS and PROPHETS were anointed: and as SOLOMON was anointed king by ZADOK the priest and NATHAN the prophet, so be you anointed.'

(viii) *The Presenting of the Spurs and Sword.*

(ix) *The Investing with the Royal Robe, and the Delivery of the Orb.*

(x) *The Investiture.*

(xi) *The Putting on of the Crown,* after which the choir sing: 'Be strong and of a good courage: keep the COMMANDMENTS of the Lord, and walk in His ways.'

(xii) *The Benediction.*

(xiii) *The Enthroning.* Then shall the Queen go to her throne (not the Chair with the Stone under the seat on which she was anointed)... and the Archbishop, standing before the Queen, shall say: 'Stand firm, and hold fast from henceforth the seat and state of royal and imperial dignity, which is this day delivered unto you, IN THE NAME AND BY THE AUTHORITY OF ALMIGHTY GOD, and by the hands of us the Bishops and servants of God Almighty, whose minister we are, and the stewards of HIS MYSTERIES, establish your Throne in righteousness, that it may stand fast FOR EVERMORE, Amen.'

Why have the MYSTERIES of the ancient Israel ceremony been so closely followed throughout? The author has emphasised the various phrases by using small capitals; and in this last act the words are identical with those used concerning David, King of Israel:

'... I have found DAVID my servant; with my HOLY OIL have I ANOINTED him... Once have I sworn by my holiness that I will not lie unto DAVID. HIS SEED shall ENDURE FOR EVER, and his THRONE AS THE SUN BEFORE ME. It shall be established FOR EVER' (*Psalm* 89:3-37).

(xiv) *The Homage.* Just as at the anointing of Saul: Then Samuel... kissed him, and said, Is it not because the Lord hath anointed thee to be captain over His inheritance? (I *Samuel* 10:1), so in the present ceremony the instructions are: Then shall the Archbishop kiss the Queen's right hand.

(xv) *The Conclusion of the Communion Service.*

To the cynic it must appear as if the tradition of the Stone has bewitched us; but let it be re-emphasised: these records do not seek to prove the verity of the traditions, there is no proof, as yet, otherwise there would be no mystery; nevertheless, he would indeed be a bold man, as well as a foolish one, who claimed they are but worthless fables.

The Stone, vibrant with both history and mystery, will remain, as it has done for countless centuries, unaffected by the scorn of the cynics, the precious heirloom of our Royal House and of our nation. It is our misfortune if we cannot see, as Canon Murray puts it, 'the veil of the eternal through the temporal,' for was it not this 'veil of the eternal' that was lifted when Jacob beheld the vision and received the promises while resting his head on the Stone?

CHAPTER III

THE RETURN OF THE STONE
TO SCOTLAND

BY MICHAEL A. CLARK

IT might well have been thought that the Stone, resident in Westminster Abbey for seven centuries, would never again be moved. Yet it was at the behest of the then Scottish Secretary, Michael Forsyth, in the Conservative Administration of Prime Minister John Major, that the Stone was returned to Scotland on the back of devolution, 700 hundred years from 1296 when it was brought to Westminster Abbey. In the opinion of many a unique medieval artefact was vandalized for a mere political gesture.

The announcement was made by John Major in the House of Commons on July 3, 1996, to effect, that with Her Majesty's 'agreement,' the Stone would be going back to Scotland, but would be returned to the Abbey for the next Coronation Service. Accordingly, at 7.00 am on November 14, 1996, which by coincidence happened to be the 48th birthday of Charles, Prince of Wales, the Stone emerged from the Abbey to set out on its journey to Scotland and Edinburgh Castle in time for St Andrew's day.

A decade later an article by the political editor of the *Scotland on Sunday* newspaper, Eddie Barnes, indicates little enthusiasm from the Royal Family:

'Remarkable new documents have revealed how...the royals battled to distance themselves from the grand return to Scotland of the ancient stone...The papers show how Conservative politicians tried and failed to get the Queen, Prince Charles or "at least" the Princess Royal to attend the glittering ceremony in Edinburgh, eventually settling for the Duke of York. Buckingham Palace was deeply concerned that the triumphal return of the stone after exactly 700 years might become an overtly political event, the documents reveal... The Conservative government was in its dying days and the then Scottish Secretary, Michael Forsyth, viewed the stone's return as something of a coup. Government papers and correspondence obtained by this newspaper show the Royal Family – and even Forsyth's boss in London, the Prime Minister [John Major] – were less than convinced…A memo from a meeting on August 30 [1996] reveals discussions between a Scottish minister and Sir Robert Fellowes, the Queen's then private secretary.

"Recent contacts with Sir Robert Fellowes suggested that the palace wished to be distanced from the various events," the minute declares… Several reasons for the royals' apparently dim view of the proceedings across the Border are put forward within the papers, as civil servants' frantic attempts to smooth the constitutional waters continued.

'A memo on September 26 by the then permanent secretary of the Scottish Office, Russell Hillhouse, declares: "The palace was somewhat disturbed by the strength of the reactions to the original announcement, though he [Fellowes] conceded things now seemed to be pretty calm."… The Queen's personal views of the return of the stone remain a mystery. All that is mentioned in the papers is one letter from Fellowes to Downing Street, in which he notes that the Queen "made no demur" over the plans.' [65]

A CONSTITUTIONAL CONFLICT WAS INITIATED

What the Queen might well have said is that to remove 'Lia Fail,' or the Stone of Destiny, from its historic resting place in Westminster – a place of sacred assembly from Druidic times – demonstrated the most serious lack of understanding by the Prime Minister concerning what the Stone represents to the realm and to the Queen's government.

The Dean and Chapter of Westminster Abbey, shocked and dismayed at the decision, more truly reflected the Queen's real views in the matter. Leading scholars in medieval history also challenged the authority of the Queen and the Prime Minister to remove the Stone from the Abbey. There was not a little anger among them at what was regarded as a low-grade political gimmick by the Prime Minister.

A highly significant and carefully worded statement was issued by the Dean and Chapter of Westminster Abbey. Constitutional experts agreed that it was inconceivable that prior approval had not been given by Buckingham Palace. It stated:

---

[65] BARNES, E. (Political Ed.) 'The Royals who ran from romancing the Stone', in *Scotland on Sunday* May 7, 2006.

'The Queen is Visitor of Westminster Abbey and therefore we accept her decision. But, as the successors of those Abbots of Westminster and Deans and Chapters who have been guardians of the Stone for so many centuries, we must urge those advising the Queen to take full account of the symbolic and emotional significance of the Stone, its integral connection with the Coronation Chair made in 1301 to contain it, and its intimate association with the sacrament of coronation.

'The Stone should not be regarded as a secular museum piece and its religious associations should be respected in decisions about its future location.'

Dr Christopher Wilson, who taught at University College, London, said:

'The Coronation Chair is one of the most important pieces of medieval furniture surviving in the country, designed on the grandest scale and gilded and painted. The Stone forms part of its unique mystery.

'Edward I may have taken the Stone from Scotland, but the important point is that James VI of Scotland, when crowned as James I, adopted the Abbey as the seat of the combined monarchy and had himself buried in the Henry VII chapel so the new dynasty was well and truly implanted in the Abbey.'

THE SYMBOL IS OF THE STONE THAT THE BUILDERS REJECTED

The concept of the Prime Minister and government of the day, that a mere change of location was all that was involved, and was not in any way significant to the authority of government, simply cannot be entertained. The Stone is of far greater symbolic significance to our heritage and its origin than politicians of the present day have been schooled to understand.

Israel from the beginning was the Stone Kingdom of God upon Earth. The Stone is symbolic of our nationhood from those biblical times. It rests in what, in effect, is our Zion: the centre of authority or 'The Queen-in-Parliament under God.' It is nothing less than the anointed foundation of government authority which, because of the anointing, *remains* Divinely appointed.

As in the case of all the European legislation since 1972, the Queen has been what at law is described as being 'Deceived in her Grant.' What has been done in the name of the Queen in removing the Stone from the spiritual and covenanted seat of government, established by a constitutional statute of the Realm, is tantamount to sending the Ark of the Covenant away from Jerusalem as a worthless secular relic. In symbolism, it is as if the Glory of the Lord has departed from the body-politic of our historic and sovereign united kingdom. An empty shell is all that remains, as is now increasingly evident as more and more power drains away from Westminster to the European Union in Brussels. It is not insignificant that the Major Administration, which removed the Stone from the seat of government at Westminster, was itself removed from power within the year.

WE SUFFER WHEN WE REJECT THE AUTHOR OF OUR WELLBEING

The Coronation Chair is not symbolic of the throne in government without the Stone. If the Stone is not present at Westminster, the seal of the covenant between the Monarch and the People is removed. The Stone is far more important, as a symbol of the Crown under God, than is the Mace to the House of Commons which must be in place in the Chamber for business to proceed. It means that we are ruled increasingly by the Will of Man, or the 'overmighty subject' – in effect, a dictatorship. Many consider the United Kingdom has been so ruled ever since we were taken by stealth into the political European Union under the Treaty of Rome – that great pagan city where the 'instruments of ratification' of the constitutional Lisbon Treaty were deposited on July 16, 2008.

The Queen's first minister should be in no doubt that with the Stone of Destiny no longer residing in the Sanctuary, as the very symbol of God's House in our midst (*Genesis* 28:22), a light has gone out in the Queen's Realm. That is having great bearing on the peace of this, our 'Jerusalem.' Indeed, on the ability of any Administration to govern with authority, be that spiritual, moral or lawful.

Our present Monarch is the only hereditary member of the Royal Family remaining in Parliament, but she is also the only living person to have been anointed by covenant oath seated upon the Stone of Destiny. To whom do ministers in Church and State and 'the host' of our Armed Forces owe their Oath of Allegiance, if not to H.M. The Queen? Elizabeth II is now the longest reigning British monarch and in 2017 is working with her thirteenth prime minister. If ever there was a moment for the nation to find itself once more and its reason for being, this surely is *that* moment.

PART II THE GARMENTS OF DESTINY

CHAPTER I

OTHER STONES

PART I followed as closely as possible the probable history of the Stone and the historical references to its people, namely, the references to a stone in the biblical story of Jacob-Israel and his seed; the references to migrations of either the Stone itself or of the people to whom it would have been a precious heirloom, by historians; the national ceremonies at which the Stone or stones have been used; the national distress at the possibility of its loss; and the dramatic precautions taken to prevent such a catastrophe when the country is at war.

There are, however, other historical records which must be taken into consideration, including those which, though they are not closely connected with the story of the Stone, have a definite bearing on the probability that the traditions attached to it have a much wider scope and foundation than the mere story which includes the Stone.

We must consider the ancient custom of using stones for ceremonial occasions, and mention some of the stones that still exist. We must also remember that Jacob's Stone in itself would have been of no intrinsic or historical value had it been merely Jacob's pillow on some occasion when he slept undisturbed in the open. The chief importance of the Stone with its tradition is the fact that, while using it as his pillow, he had a dream or vision, during which he had serious and far-reaching promises made to him by God; thus, the expected fulfilment of these promises would be the reason for it being treated reverently by Jacob, and for it remaining a valued and precious symbolic possession to his seed.

The many customs which were common to the people of Israel in their early Palestinian days, and the traditions attached to their national emblems and ceremonies in the days of their glory, would, most likely, as so often happens to peoples, become more desirable to them the further away they wandered from their native land – a form of nostalgia.

Some records of the migrations of these people to Spain, Ireland and Scotland have already been given because tradition confirms that during these migrations the Stone also was transferred; but other records and other traditions can be considered which bring to light similar customs and ceremonies performed by people arriving in this country by other routes; whether all these separate migrations have an intimate connection must be left to reasonable judgment.

THE WISDOM OF THE DRUIDS

According to E.O. Gordon, 'The "King's Bench" in the great Judgement Halls of Winchester and Westminster, to which the kings of England were formerly "lifted" before proceeding to their coronation, is said to trace back to the ancient practice at Abury of placing the King on a stone sedd or seat within the precincts of the "Supreme Seat," or "High Court" after that, by the "Voice of the People" he had been "Elected." ' [66]

Abury was the pre-Christian Metropolitan Circle of the Druids. It is customary to think of the Druids as a primitive sun-worshipping people, who came to these Islands about 1800 BC under Hu Gadarn, but their Triads, of which there are many still extant, give an entirely different picture; here are three of the Triads, cited in *Prehistoric London*, upon which we may form our own judgment:

'God consists necessarily of Three things:
the Greatest of Life;
the Greatest of Knowledge;
and the Greatest of Power,
and of what is the Greatest there can be no more than One of anything.'

'In every person there is a soul,
In every soul there is intelligence:
In every intelligence there is thought,
In every thought there is either good or evil:
In every evil there is death:
In every good there is life,
In every life there is God.'

'Grant, O God, thy Protection;
And in Protection, Strength;
And in Strength, Understanding;
And in Understanding, Knowledge;
And Knowledge, the Knowledge of Justice;
And in the Knowledge of Justice, the Love of it;

---

[66] GORDON, E.O. *Prehistoric London*. London: Covenant Publishing Company Ltd., 1932, 3rd edition, pp. 58, 59.

And in that Love, the Love of all Existences;
And in the Love of all Existences, the Love of God.
God, and all Goodness.'[67]

Diogenes Laertius, who lived about 220 BC, affirms that 'the Druids among the Britons were the same as the Philosophers among the Greeks, the Magi among the Persians...;' [68] and the *Pictorial History of England* states:

> 'Among the Celtic nations Britain seems to have had the character of a sort of Holy Land, and to have been the centre of the Druids.' [69]

In the Druidical language the syllables Ton, Tor and Tot conveyed the meaning 'sacred,' and we find them in place names all over England, such as in Tonbridge, Torquay and Totnes. London is said to have been built on and around four Druidical Mounds, and we have to-day the relics of these names: Tothill, which is represented to-day by Tothill Street across from Westminster Abbey; Penton, which is perpetuated in the name Pentonville, a district which lies behind the stations St. Pancras and King's Cross; the Bryn Gwyn (Bryn = hill, Gwyn = white or holy) where now stands the White Tower of the Tower of London; and the Llanin (llan = sacred, din = eminence) now Parliament Hill, Hampstead Heath. One of several suggestions is that Llandin may be the origin of the name London. [70]

BRUTUS THE TROJAN AND HIS STONE

Brutus, the Trojan, was famed in their Triads as one of the 'Three King Revolutionists of Britain,' and it is he who was the reputed founder of London in the early centuries BC.

The Story of Brutus is, according to Professor L. A. Waddell, fully confirmed; in his *Phoenician Origin of Britons, Scots and Anglo-Saxons* he states:

> 'Now this earlier portion of the Chronicles (The Ancient British Chronicles) records circumstantially the first arrival of the Britons by sea, in Albion under "King Brut-the-Trojan" ... and his

[67] ibid. pp. 43; 41; 177.
[68] BAYLEY, H. *The Lost Language of London.* London: Jonathan Cape, 1935, p. 251.
[69] KNIGHT, CHARLES. *Pictorial History of England.* London: SDUK, 1837, p. 25.
[70] GORDON, op.cit. Chapters 1-3.

colonisation and first civilisation of the land... This tradition, we shall now find, is fully established by a mass of new historical facts and associated evidence.' [71]

Brutus was the great grandson of Aeneas, and Professor Sayce, the archaeologist, in writing a preface to *Ilios* by Schliemann, another archaeologist, says:

'Thanks to the discoveries in unearthing the remains of Ilium, we know who the Trojans originally were; that they belonged to the Aryan family; so that we, as well as the Greeks, can hail the subjects of Priam, King of Troy, as brethren in blood and speech.' [72]

What were their religious beliefs? Professor Waddell, in his preface to the above work, says:

'In Religion, it is now found that the exalted religion of the Aryan Phoenicians, the so-called "Sun-worship", with its lofty ethics and belief in a future life with resurrection from the dead, was widely prevalent in early Britain down to the Christian era.' [73]

At Totnes, on the river Dart, which is the oldest port in Devon, there is a granite boulder in the street which leads up from the river, and over this boulder is a sign: 'This is Brutus' Stone.' The tradition is that it was on this stone that Brutus 'set foot' when he landed in Britain, and the importance attached to its tradition is shown by the fact that it has been used for the proclamation of kings in the past; the proclamation of King George V on May 6, 1910, was made by the Mayor of Totnes while standing on this stone.

The Marquess of Bute notes:

'In the *Proceedings of the Society of Antiquaries of Scotland,* under the date of December 9, 1878, there is printed a paper by the late Captain F. W. L. Thomas, R.N., intituled *Dunadd, Glassary, Argylshire; The Place of Inauguration of the Dalriadic Kings.* The object of the paper is to call attention to the fact that

---

[71] WADDELL, L.A. *The Phoenician Origin of Britons, Scots & Anglo Saxons.* London: Williams & Norgate, 1925. p.142.
[72] SCHLIEMANN, HEINRICH. *Ilios: The City and Country of the Trojans.* London: John Murray, 1880.
[73] WADDELL, op.cit. preface.

near the highest part of Dunadd, the ancient fortified hill in the midst of the Moss of Crinan, which is now recognised as having been the citadel of the early kings of the Dalriadic Scots, there is engraven upon the rock the representation of a human footprint. This sculptured impression, says Captain Thomas, does not show such a mark as would be made by a naked foot, "but such as would be made when the foot is clothed by a thick stocking or *curan*. The engravure is for the right foot."' [74]

The Marquess then goes on to enumerate (p. 2) many other such stones, including one each at Carmyllie, Forfarshire; Glenesk; Broch of Clickemin, Shetland; North Yell, Shetland; on the Clare hills near Dromandoora; on the hill of Lech near Monaghan; and a stone with two footprints at St. Columba's Stone, at Belmont, Londonderry; and at Lady Kirk, Orkney. There are, he says, also divers foreign examples, especially one by the shore of the creek Croesty, in the commune of Arzo, Morbihan, Brittany.

The idea seems to have been that the taking of the vows of inauguration while standing on a stone typified the steadfastness of the intention to keep these vows.

The strangest and most interesting record concerning Brutus, as far as it concerns the traditions of the Coronation Stone, is one from *The Historia Regum Britanniae*, by Geoffrey of Monmouth:

> 'And when Brutus had finished the building of the city (London) and had strengthened it with walls and castles, he consecrated them and made inflexible laws for the government of such as should dwell there peacefully, and he put protection on the city and granted privilege to it. At the time, Beli the Priest ruled in Judea, and the Ark of the Covenant was in captivity to the Philistines.' [75]

What had Beli the Priest of Israel and the Ark of the Covenant to do with Brutus and his records, unless there were some connection between his people and the Israelites?

It would seem then that these Islands were colonised at an early date by people from Palestine, Egypt and Greece; and just as even in these days our own people follow in a steady stream to the lands where their

[74] BUTE, op.cit p.1.
[75] GEOFFREY OF MONMOUTH. *Historia Regum Britannia*. Trans. R. E. Jones. London: Longman, 1929 p. 172.

kinsmen have settled, so those early settlers may have attracted various migrations of their people to these Islands throughout the centuries.

Tradition has it that Brutus also brought a stone to Britain; there was an old saying: 'So long as the Stone of Brutus is safe, so long shall London flourish.' [76] One belief is that the Stone was originally laid on the altar of the Temple of Diana by Brutus, for it was Diana who prophesied that he (Brutus) should reign in Britain, and it is thought that at one time a temple to Diana stood where St. Paul's Cathedral now stands.

'LONDON STONE'

There is also to be seen a stone behind iron bars in a wall opposite Cannon Street Station, in the City of London, called the 'London Stone'; it is merely an old Roman mile stone, but this idea is discounted by the fact that Stow, the antiquarian, says that 'the London Stone was mentioned in a "faire written Gospel booke given to Christes Church in Canterburie by Ethelstane King of the West Saxons",' and the first mayor of London is described in the *Liberde Antiquis legibus* as 'Henricus filius Eylwini de London-stane'; a mile stone would hardly achieve such fame as to be included in historical records.

E. O. Gordon quotes Sir Lawrence Gomme, who thinks that, 'like other great stones, it most likely marked the place where open-air assemblies gathered to legislate for the community'; and another writer (Brayley) as saying: 'Some, however, hold this venerable relic was regarded with a sort of superstitious zeal, and, like the Palladium of Troy, the fate and safety of the city was imagined to depend on its preservation.' [77]

In Kenyon's translation of Aristotle's *Athenian Constitution* we find: 'and the nine Archons made oath upon the stone' [78] and, quoting Saxo Grammaticus,

> 'the ancients, when they were to choose a king, were wont to stand on stones planted in the ground, and to proclaim their votes, in order to foreshadow from the steadfastness of the stones that the deed would be lasting.'[79]

---

[76] SPENCE, L. *Legendary London: Early London in Tradition and History*. London: R. Hale & Co., 1937. p. 171.
[77] GORDON, op.cit. p.11.
[78] ARISTOTLE. *Athenian Constitution*. Trans. Sir F. Kenyon. London: G. Bell & Sons, 1914. Sect. 1, part 7.
[79] *The Nine Books of the Danish History of Saxo Grammaticus*. Trans. Elton, et al. New York: Norroena Society, 1905. p.39.

THE SAXON CORONATION STONE

All these traditions of stones being used by some ancient people at ceremonies in connection with their kings lead us to Kingston-on-Thames, where, surrounded by an iron railing, there is a stone on which seven of the Anglo-Saxon kings were crowned after their arrival in England. [80]

The people of these Saxon kings brought the custom with them when they migrated to this Island. The Franks crowned their kings over a stone; Charlemagne was crowned upon the 'Marmorne Stuhl'. [81] The Swedish kings were crowned at Uppsala on a sacred stone:

> 'The ancient law of Sweden says: "When we have lost a king of these lands then shall each Laghman... summon twelve men, wary and wise. With them shall he come into the Stone of Mora and choose a king... In each land and shore shall the King promise and vow to keep the oath which he swore at the Stone of Mora, when he was first elected king," '

and in Denmark: 'The Kings of Denmark were crowned in a circle of stones.' [82] Is it not strange that in these countries, Germany, France, Sweden and Denmark, the custom is no longer maintained, yet here in Britain it is still a national ceremony?

FROM THE MIDDLE EAST TO THE BRITISH ISLES

The stones to which particular attention has already been drawn have been single stones used for some special purpose, mostly for the crowning of kings, but there are other stones forming Circles, Cromlechs, Dolmens, etc., which mark the migrations of peoples whose starting-place was likewise Egypt and Palestine, and showing by their existence to-day a similar route of migration.

The simplest and most convincing way to give an idea of the places of origin of the peoples whose custom it was to erect stones, their westward trail, and their final destination in these Islands, is to quote several different authorities on the subject.

---

[80] Kingston, or king's tun or farmstead, was already a royal demesne in AD 838. Edward the Elder was the first king to be crowned on the stone in AD 900. See LEWIS, SAMUEL *A Topographical History of England.* [online] Available at British History Online.

[81] A marble chair.

[82] STACPOOLE, op.cit. p. 65.

Major H. S. Palmer points out that 'the remains described are nearly identical in character with those which in England and Scotland are commonly called Druidic Circles.' [83]

Professor Sayce explains that a dolichocephalic race, akin to the 'Amorites', was responsible for the chain of cromlechs reaching from Britain, through Spain, and North Africa, to Palestine. [84]

Dean Stanley draws attention to the fact that the stone circles in Britain find their counterpart in the land of Israel. [85]

Professor L. A. Waddell, LLD., C.B., writes:

'These early "prehistoric" exploiters of the Tin, Copper, Gold and Lead mines, and Jet and Amber trades, appear to have been floating colonies of merchant seamen and adventurers, who at first occupied strategic islets on peninsular seaports off-lying the chief native trade marts or mines, such as the Phoenicians usually selected for defensive purposes in most of their colonies, on the model of Tyre, Sidon, Acre, Aradus, Carthage and Gades (or Cadiz). Of such a character are Ictis or St. Michael's Mount, Wight, Gower, the Aran isles off Galway, Dun Barton, Inch Keith, etc. Later they established themselves inland in the hinterland of their ports, as evidenced by their Stone Circles and other rude megalith monuments....' [86]

In *Stonehenge and Other British Stone Monuments Astronomically Considered*, Sir Norman Lockyer remarks:

'It is interesting to note that, while the astronomical side of the enquiry suggests a close connection with Egyptian thought, the folklore and traditions, when studied in relation with the monuments, indicate a close connection between the ancient British and the Semitic civilisations...' [87]

---

[83] PALMER, MAJOR H.S. *Ancient History from the Monuments: Sinai*. London: Christian Knowledge Society, 1878. pp. 102-3.
[84] SAYCE, A.H. *The Hittites: The Story of a Forgotten Empire*. 4th ed. London: Religious Tract Society, 1925. p. 19.
[85] STANLEY, DEAN A.P. *Sinai and Palestine*. 5th ed. London: John Murray, 1858. p. 277.
[86] WADDELL, op.cit. p. 366.
[87] LOCKYER, SIR NORMAN. *Stonehenge and Other British Stone Monuments Astronomically Considered*. 2nd ed. London: Macmillan, 1909. p. 478.

Finally, in '*Abury*' William Stukeley, F.R.S., antiquarian, writes:

'When I first began these studies about the Druid antiquities, I plainly discern'd the religion profess'd in these places (the Druidic Circles) was the first, simple, patriarchal, religion.' [88]

Again, as with the single stones, let us note the strange, even significant, fact that while these circles, etc., still exist along the route of migration as ancient monuments, only in Britain does there still exist a body of Druids who periodically gather in the ancient ceremonial garb to hold their Eisteddfod.

[88] STUKELEY. WILLIAM. *Abury: A Temple of the British Druids*. London, 1743. preface. p. i.

CHAPTER II

PEOPLES AND CUSTOMS

FROM whence came all these people with their customs? Let us tabulate them:

(1) The Saxons, whose previous location was what is now known as Germany.

(2) The Franks, who dominated Gaul, which was then the major part of Western Europe.

(3) The Swedes, whose land was the peninsula now occupied by Norway and Sweden.

(4) The Scots, whom King Robert the Bruce claimed came from Scythia, which lay in the region of the Caucasus Mountains.

(5) The Trojans, whom Professor Waddell claims came to Britain in 1103 BC with Brutus, from Greece.

(6) The Greeks, who through Gathelus are claimed by Boece and others to have come here even earlier.

(7) People from Egypt, who are designated by Irish *MS 'Kings of the Race of Eibhear'.*

(8) The People of Israel, the House of David, and Gathelus, who are mentioned in *Dialogo della Musica Antica,* [89] *The Kings of the Race of Eibhear,* [90] and by Dr. Isaac da Costa in his *Israel and the Gentiles.* [91]

MIGRATIONS BY LAND AND SEA

One or two extracts from authoritative historians may help to give an idea of the movements of peoples over the centuries, and over the continent of Europe.

In the notes on his translation of George Buchanan's *History of Scotland*, Aikman writes :

'Gothini – the Goths of the moderns, the Getae or Getes of the ancients, the same people, Mr. Pinkerton thinks, as the Scythians. In his Dissertation, he traces their progress from Modern Persia, upward, over the river Araxes in Armenia, and

---

[89] GALILEI, op. cit.
[90] KEATING, op.cit.
[91] DA COSTA, op.cit.

the mountains of the Causcasus, into little, or ancient Scythia, on the Euxine. Thence they spread, he supposes, into Thrace, Greece, Illyricum, Dacia, Germany and Scandinavia. From Scandinavia they proceeded to Scotland, Jutland and the Danish Isles. From Germany to Gaul, and Spain and Italy... and he does so upon the authority of Caesar, and the other ancient writers whom he quotes, who wrote before the language of Europe had been changed by the new swarms from the north, that overturned the Roman empire, and settled in the half depopulated provinces, and who derived their information immediately from the Gauls, and their colonies. But both statements establish the same material point – the identity of the Gauls, with numerous tribes scattered over extensive and distant countries, and Tacitus affirms that the Gothini spoke the language of the Gauls...' [92]

The German anthropologist, Hans Gunther, observes in *Racial Elements of European History*:

'The investigations into the traces left behind them by that widespread Nordic people, the Sacae (Scythians) with its many tribes, are well worthy of attention... The ancient writers (such as Polemon of Illium, Galienos, Clement of Alexandria, Adamantios) state that the Sacae were like the Kelts and Germans, and describe them as fair, or ruddy fair.' [93]

Whilst in 1743 William Stukeley affirmed: 'Likewise I have open'd a large communication between the patriarchal family, of Abraham particularly, and of the first planters of the coasts on the ocean of Spain, Gaul, Germany and Britain.' [94]

Moreover, the famous Jewish historian, Josephus, writing in AD 70, seems to have had knowledge of the beginning of the migrations of most of his people from Asia towards Europe for, in his *Antiquities of the Jews*, he writes:

'... wherefore there are but two tribes in Asia and Europe subject to the Romans, while the ten tribes are beyond the

[92]BUCHANAN, op.cit. Vol.i, book ii, p.81. (notes)
[93] GÜNTHER, H. *Racial Elements of European History*. Trans. G.C. Wheeler. London: Methuen & Co., 1927. p.130.
[94] STUKELEY, op.cit. preface, p. ii.

Euphrates till now (AD 70) and are an immense multitude, and not to be estimated by numbers.' [95]

One cannot but note that, whatever may be the true story of the Stone, the people, whom tradition claims to have been the inheritors of the promises given to their ancestor while using the Stone as a pillow, can be traced in various migrations from Egypt, Greece and Spain to Ireland and Scotland, and over the Continent of Europe from old-time Scythia, Greece, Gaul, Germany and the Scandinavian countries to England and Scotland.

Even ancient art adds its evidence, for George Bain, an acknowledged authority on Celtic Art, affirms:

> 'The evidences now available show that most aspects of Celtic art had arrived and had matured in Britain and Ireland many centuries before the Romans came, and that the peoples who brought them had made contacts in their migrations with the people who had built and lived in the city of Ur... and with the tribes that later became the makers of the Greek Empire. Migrations via the Mediterranean, the Baltic, and overland Europe entered Britain and Ireland and mingled in the birth of British and the Irish Celtic art long before the dawn of British history.' [96]

That their custom of using a stone on which to crown their kings should be followed by the people of the various migrations is not so strange, but that the custom should survive only at their final destination is more curious and suggestive, and although, because of the foibles of human nature, many superstitions and claims may have been attached to the various Stones throughout the centuries, no claims are attached to the Coronation Stone except that it is the precious heirloom of the 'People of Jacob,' because of its being the Stone on which he rested his head when he had his dream concerning the distant future of his multitudinous seed.

---

[95] JOSEPHUS, FLAVIUS. *Antiquities of the Jews.* Book xi, ch.v.
[96] BAIN, GEORGE. 'Celtic art: the methods of construction.' In *Scotland's S.M.T. Magazine* 40:4, 1947. pp.33-8.

THE WITNESS OF THE LAW.

What is equally strange is that many of the customs and traditions of the 'People of the Stone' have also been preserved among us till the present day. Lord Chief Justice Coke, in his preface to Volume iii of his *Pleadings*, says: 'The original laws of this land were composed of such elements as Brutus first selected from the ancient Greek and Trojan institutions.' [97]

That the Law of Moses is still considered the supreme guide for the law of our land is testified by the Archbishop of Canterbury at the crowning of our King, for, as already mentioned, on presenting the King with a copy of the Bible he uses these very words: 'Here is wisdom, this is the Royal Law; these are the lively Oracles of God.'

Even in the architectural scheme of our Royal Courts of Justice in the Strand, London, there are figures in stone of those to whom we owe our inheritance of just government and equity in our national life. On a pinnacle overlooking Carey Street, which runs parallel with the Strand, at the back of the Law Courts, is the figure of Moses, the great Israel leader, who received the Law from God. Facing the Strand there are three figures on elevated points, the central figure being Christ, Who stated, when speaking of that same Law: 'Think not that I am come to destroy the law, or the prophets; I am not come to destroy, but to fulfil. For verily I say unto you, Till heaven and earth pass, one jot or one tittle shall in no wise pass from the law, till all be fulfilled' (*Matthew* 5:17, 18). On His right is King Solomon, who is still considered to have been one of the wisest kings, and who administered this Law over Israel during the period of their greatest prosperity and happiness. On the left is the figure of King Alfred, of whom Dr. Pauli, in *The Life of King Alfred*, writes:

'It would be difficult to find in any other collection of laws of the middle ages so large a portion of Bible matter as in this; and we know too, that no other has so completely adopted the principles of the Mosaic Law.' [98]

---

[97] COKE, SIR EDWARD (1549 – 1634). This reference can be found in *The Selected Writings of Sir Edward Coke in 3 Volumes* ed. Steve Sheppard. Indianapolis: Liberty Fund, 2003.
[98] PAULI, REINHOLD. *König Ælfred und seine Stelle in der Geschichte Englands (The Life of King Alfred)*. Eds. Pauli and Thomas Wright. London, 1852. p. 136.

THE SACRED TENTH OR TITHE

When Jacob set up 'the pillar' or 'Stone' and anointed it, he made the oath: 'And this stone, which I have set for a pillar, shall be God's house: and of all that thou shalt give me I will surely give the tenth unto thee.'

Tithing was still in existence as a system of dues in our land up to 1977, although the 'Tithe Commutation Act of 1936' and the 'Tithe Act of 1891' altered the method of payment. *The Harmsworth Encyclopaedia,* under 'Tithes,' gives:

> 'Tithes were originally a payment of a tenth of such things as annually increase or render annual crop, i.e. grain and fruit; mixed tithes, e.g. the young of animals, milk, etc.; and personal tithes, or gain arising from labour. They were paid to the clergyman, except in extra-parochial places, where they were paid to the King. By the Tithes Commutation Acts of 1936, and the Tithes Act of 1891, nearly all tithes have been commuted into a tithe rent charge.' [99]

THE WITNESS OF THE PRAYER BOOK

The Prayer Book of the Church of England, although published originally in AD 1549, states in its preface that, with the exception of minor alterations, it is the same as the original service books; also, according to *British Reformers*:

> 'At this time (AD 1549) Archbishop Cranmer asserted before Parliament that the Prayer Book which he asked might be authorised by that body for general use in the Church of England were the same prayers which had been in use in Britain for over fifteen hundred years.... "I will by God's grace defend not only the common prayers of the Church, but also the doctrine and religion set out by our said Sovereign Lord, King Edward VI, to be more pure and according to God's Word than any other that has been in use in England these thousand years. The same doctrine and usage is to be followed which was in the Church fifteen hundred years past, and we shall prove that the order of the Church set out at this present in this realm by Act of Parliament is the same as was used in the Church fifteen hundred years past." ' [100]

---

[99] HAMMERTON. op.cit. Tithes in Great Britain were terminated by the Finance Act 1977.
[100] STOKES, GEORGE. *Lives of the British Reformers, from Wickliff to Fox Vol.VIII.* London: Religious Tract Society, 1832. p. 271.

That repeated statement, 'Fifteen hundred years past,' taken from the time of its declaration AD 1549, brings us to AD 49, and this supports the statement of Gildas the ancient historian (AD 516-570):

> 'We certainly know that Christ, the True Son, afforded His Light, the knowledge of His precepts, to our Island in the last year of the reign of Tiberios Caesar.' [101]

It should be borne in mind that this last year of the reign of Tiberius Caesar was AD 37. Note also Sir Henry Spelman's words, in his *Concilia*:

> 'We have abundant evidence that this Britain of ours received the Faith, and that from the disciples of Christ Himself, soon after the Crucifixion.' [102]

The Prayer Book throughout its order of service is a continual reminder of the Covenants made with the forefathers Abraham, Isaac and Jacob, and who are claimed as OUR forefathers.

In the *Benedictus* we sing: 'To perform the mercy promised to OUR FOREFATHERS; and to remember His holy Covenant; to perform the OATH which He sware to OUR FOREFATHER ABRAHAM: that He would give us...'

In the *Magnificat* we sing: 'He remembering His mercy hath holpen His servant ISRAEL: as He promised to OUR FOREFATHERS, ABRAHAM and HIS SEED, for ever.'

In the *Cantate* we thank God for remembering 'His mercy and truth toward the HOUSE OF ISRAEL.'

In the Te Deum we pray: 'O Lord, save THY PEOPLE: and bless THINE HERITAGE.'

In the *Nunc Dimittis* we sing: 'Mine eyes have seen thy salvation, which thou hast prepared... to be a light to lighten the Gentiles: and to be the glory of THY PEOPLE ISRAEL.'

In the *Jubilate* we declare: 'We are HIS PEOPLE, and the sheep of His pasture.'

While in the *Responses* we use the terms: 'Thy People,' 'Thy Chosen,' 'Thine Inheritance,' all terms used in olden times of the people

---

[101] GILDAS (surnamed "Sapiens", or The Wise) (516-570). *Liber querulous de exidio Britanniae. On the Ruin of Britain* Translated by Giles, J.A. London: Henry G. Bohn, 1848. Sct. 8, p. 25.
[102] SPELMAN, SIR HENRY (?1564 – 1641) *Concilia, Decreta, Leges, Constitutiones, in re Ecclesiarum Orbis Britannici.* 2 vols. London: R. Badger /P. Stephani & C. Meredith, 1639-64. fol. p. 1.

of Israel to whom the Covenants were given. Let us remember that these prayers, according to Archbishop Cranmer's statement before Parliament in 1549, are the same as were in use in AD 49 at which time, according to Gildas and Sir Henry Spelman, the disciples of Christ were preaching the Gospel in Britain.

It is strange that the traditions of both the Stone, and the people who are the guardians of it, should point to the same source, and cynicism towards the import of the probable reason will not remove the continued existence or use of the traditions. It is merely playing the ostrich, and thus missing much that may help us, in the words of Canon Murray, 'to see the veil of the eternal through the temporal.'

WESTMINSTER ABBEY

The home of the Stone for the last 650 years has been the Sanctuary in Westminster Abbey, where the crowning of our Kings takes place. The site on which the Abbey stands was, in ancient times, an island, Thorney Island, on which stood a Druidic Circle. In the Abbey is the tomb of Sebert, King of the East Saxons who, it is believed, founded the first church (c. 616), but the proof of the existence of a church in 788 can be seen in the Chapter House where there is a Charter of King Offa of Mercia granting lands and privileges to the Church of St. Peter 'at Thorney,' the official title of the Abbey being 'The Collegiate Church of St. Peter Westminster.'

The Abbey as we know it to-day was founded by Edward the Confessor (1042-66), who is buried within the building, and the first coronation to take place in the Abbey was of William the Conqueror, since when the coronations of all monarchs, with the exception of Edward V and Edward VIII (who were not crowned), have taken place there.

The West Front is the entrance through which all important processions enter; it is therefore through this doorway that a King enters for his coronation; this was the last part of the Abbey to be completed in 1517.

Over the doorway is what is known as the West Window. It is a beautiful window of Gothic design, commenced in 1735 and finished in 1745. One cannot but wonder what idea guided the authorities when choosing the subject of its illustration, for here again we are taken back to the forefathers, and the twelve sons of Jacob-Israel whose seed, according to the promises made to him in the vision, while his head rested on the

Stone, were to be 'as the dust of the earth,' who were to 'spread abroad to the west, and to the east, and to the north, and to the south,' and who were to become 'a nation and a company of nations.'

The window contains twenty-four panels in four rows: the top row, where the width of the arch is narrow, has three panels only, and the lower three rows have seven panels each. Each panel bears a representation of a full-length figure, except in the lowest row where the panels contain only three emblems.

The names of the figures in order from the top are:

Top row: Abraham, Isaac and Jacob.

Second row: Reuben, Simeon, Levi, Judah, Zebulon, Issachar and Dan.

Third row: Gad, Asher, Naphtali, Joseph, Benjamin, Moses and Aaron.

Fourth row: The emblems of Moses and Aaron and between them, as if claiming a rightful place in this family, the Arms of Britain – the Lion and the Unicorn.

According to the *Jewish Encyclopaedia*, the emblem of Judah was a 'Lion,' and of Joseph a 'Bull,' while in *Deuteronomy* 33:17, where it gives the account of Jacob's blessing to and prophecies concerning his sons, the words applying to Joseph are:

'His glory is like the firstling of his bullock, and his horns are like the horns of unicorns: with them he shall push the people together to the ends of the earth: and they are the ten thousands of Ephraim, and they are the thousands of Manasseh' (Joseph's sons).

CHAPTER III

DESTINY IN ACTION

IT may be that the tradition of the Stone being the one Jacob used at Bethel will never be proved; it may even be that the details of its migrations from Palestine through the various countries to Britain will remain an unsolved mystery; yet, the character, the national behaviour and the aspirations of the people who, for so many centuries, have been its guardians are still an enigma to people of other lands and even to themselves.

We speak, and even act, as if it were destiny that controlled us, a destiny of which we are strangely aware, yet cannot explain; a tradition which we feel in our bones, but superficially scorn, though inwardly cherish.

The effect on the outsider is expressed by many foreign authors, whether their attitude be one of friendliness or antipathy, and is summed up by the late Herr Wilhelm Dibelius, Professor of English in the University of Berlin, who lived in England for some years. The book is called *England*, and, as the author states, was written to help his people to understand 'the soul of a people,' or the soul of Britain, and its argument is embodied in these words:

> 'If there is to be world progress, the Anglo-Saxon idea must continue its missionary work in the future. It is the strenuous but glorious task of Anglo-Saxondom to stand for freedom all over the world and to draw the sword in the cause of small and oppressed nations; the development of the world will one day bring it about that the entire earth dominion (with which the United States will be associated, in some form or other) will transform itself into a league of free nations, whose defence – in so far as this may still be necessary – will be undertaken by Britain.'

But the paragraph with which he follows this statement is the most revealing:

> 'We have here more or less set out what no Briton would think of setting out systematically, or even, disliking systematic thought as he does, arrange for himself as a logical sequence of

thought, but what dominates the feeling of every Briton with the force of a Gospel.' [103]

To put forward such a scheme as a national aim would shock our national feelings of modesty and understatement, but, nevertheless, as Herr Dibelius says, it is our 'Gospel'; we are, unconsciously perhaps, in line with the Stone, for one of the promises to Jacob while resting on it was: 'In thee and in thy seed shall all the families of the earth be blessed.'

Herr Dibelius died in 1931, but had he lived he would have had confirmation of his views from speeches of the great men of our land.

Winston S. Churchill, addressing the members of both the legislative bodies of the United States at Washington on December 26, 1941, said:

'If you will allow me to use other language, I will say that he must indeed have a blind soul who cannot see that some great purpose and design is being worked out here below, of which we have the honour to be faithful servants.' [104]

Dr. Temple, Archbishop of Canterbury, at a service in St. Paul's Cathedral on September 26, 1943, declared:

'We may, and we must, believe that He who has led our fathers in ways so strange, and has preserved our land in a manner so marvellous, has a purpose for us to serve in the preparation for His perfect Kingdom. In the tradition of our nation and our Empire, we are entrusted with a treasure to be used for the welfare of mankind.'

His Majesty King George VI, broadcasting to his people on the evening of 'D Day,' 1944, said:

'We shall ask not that God may do our will, but that we may be enabled to do the will of God; and we dare to believe that God has used our nation and Empire as an instrument for fulfilling His High purpose.'

---

[103] DIBELIUS, PROF. WILHELM. *England.* London: Jonathan Cape, 1930. p. 178.
[104] Prime Minister Winston Churchill's Address to the Congress of the United States, December 26, 1941 from CHURCHILL, WINSTON S. *The Second World War Vol. III.* London: Cassell & Co. Ltd., 1950. pp.595-6.

During World War II the Ministry of Information issued leaflets for the instruction of the people. In days of physical danger and personal tragedy the cloak of materialism is thrust aside and our spiritual intuition is given freedom to function, our thoughts are deeper, and our words bolder and more courageous; it may have been these conditions that produced the leaflet dated May 6, 1943, entitled: 'The Spiritual Issues of the War,' which quoted the following words of the Bishop of Exeter:

'No one can reflect upon the past history, the slow growth, the preservation – not without some loss – of this Commonwealth of Nations without seeing in it a mighty instrument which God may use as leader of the United Nations to heal a world in ruins. If we dare to use the word "a chosen people", all boasting will be excluded if we remember that in the language of true religion "chosen" means for service, perhaps for suffering, never for favouritism. Let us therefore thank God for the new opportunity He is giving our nation and Empire.'

The tradition of the Stone tells us that Jacob was promised:

'A nation and a company of nations shall be of thee... and thou shalt spread abroad to the west, and to the east, and to the north, and to the south: and in thee and in thy seed shall all the families of the earth be blessed' (*Genesis* 35:11; 28: 14).

Lord Elton, the acknowledged historian of the British Empire, of whose writings it has been said, 'he does not neglect the moral and spiritual realities which underlie physical events', concludes his book, *Imperial Commonwealth*, with these words:

'And is not the British Empire a living example of what in the new age the world will need most – the peaceful and enduring association of free nations within a world community?... And the gift of the British Empire to the future is likely rather to be of the Empire-Commonwealth itself as the pattern, and, it may even be, the nucleus, of some wider organisation yet to be. Britain "is the single country in the world," wrote a German scholar, "that, looking after its own interest with meticulous care has at the same time something to give to others; the single country where patriotism does not represent a threat or challenge to the rest of the world; the single country that invariably summons the most progressive, idealistic and efficient forces in other nations to co-operate with it." And it may well be that the island from which the world learnt the art of freedom will yet teach it the art of unity. It may well be that her present sufferings have finally fitted Britain for that role. But history cannot read the future. All that history can say is that such an outcome would match the pattern of the past.' [105]

Truth is indeed stranger than fiction; what author, however brilliant, would have conceived the theme of a Stone which would attract to itself such traditions that it would be carried throughout the millenniums and throughout the countries as a sacred emblem of its people; used for the greatest of all ceremonies, the crowning of their kings; and weaving into the soul of its people a 'Gospel' and a vision that would shape their destiny.

'There are moments when, in the words of Lord Grey of Falloden, "there is more in the minds of events than in the minds of the chief actors." At such moments neither reason of state, as seen by the man of affairs, nor yet the various incentives of which the individual is conscious, nor even all these together, will fully account for the outburst of energy which ensues. The nation itself may be said to be responding, altogether instinctively, to impulses of which it is never consciously aware, and to laws of which as yet we know little. We may say, if we will, that destiny beckons to it. As in dreams the subconscious mind of the individual can sometimes foresee the future, so, it is possible, the subconscious mind of the nation is sometimes aware of what awaits it.' [106]

The story of the Stone and that of the people who have been its guardians are inseparable; much in both stories is incomplete, yet more historical facts would require reasonable explanation for their existence, if we were to dismiss the traditions as foolish, than there are missing links in the story of the traditions as they exist. As Lord Elton has said: 'History cannot read the future. All that history can say is that such an outcome would match the pattern of the past.'

---

[105]ELTON, LORD GODFREY. *Imperial Commonwealth*. London: Collins, 1945 pp. 522-3.
[106] ibid. pp. 31- 32.

Let us follow the advice of one of our famous writers and thinkers of the past – Francis Bacon:

> 'Read not to contradict and confute,
> not to believe and take for granted,
> but to weigh and consider –
> Histories make men wise.'

ROBERT I

m. (first) ISABEL, *d.* of DONALD, EARL of Mar.

MARJORIE *m.* WALTER, 6th High Steward of Scotland.

ROBERT II *m.* ELIZABETH, d. of

ROBERT III *m.* 1367, ANNABELLA, *d.* of JOHN DRUMMOND, of Stobhall.

JAMES I *m.* 1424, LADY JOAN BEAUFORT, *d.* of the 1st Earl of Somerset.

JAMES II *m.* 1449, MARY, *d.* of ARNOLD, Duke of Gueldres.

JAMES III *m.* 1469, MARGARET, *d.* of CHRISTIAN I, King of Denmark.

JAMES IV *m.* 1503, MARGARET, *el. d.* of KING HENRY VII of England.

JAMES V *m.* 1538, MARIE DE LORRAINE, *d.* of CLAUDE DE GUISE LORRAINE, Duke d'Aumale.

MARY *m.* 1565, HENRY, LORD Darnley, *son* of the 4th Earl of Lennox.

JAMES VI (became JAMES I of England) *m.* 1589, ANNE, *d.* of FREDERICK II, King of Denmark.

ELIZABETH *m.* 1612, FREDERICK V, Elector Palatine and King of Bohemia.

SOPHIA *m.* 1658, ERNEST, Elector of Hanover and Duke of Brunswick Luneburg.

GEORGE I *m.* 1682, SOPHIA , *d.* of GEORGE, Duke of Brunswick and Zelle.

GEORGE II *m.* 1705, CAROLINE, *d.* of the Margrave of Bradenburg-Anspach.

FREDERICK (Prince of Wales) *m.* 1736, AUGUSTA, *d.* of FREDERICK II, Duke of Saxe-Gotha.

GEORGE III *m.* 1761, CHARLOTTE SOPHIA, *d.* of the Reigning Duke of Mecklenburg-Strelitz.

EDWARD (Duke of Kent) *m.* 1818, VICTORIA, *d.* of the Duke of Saxe-Coburg-Saalfeld.

VICTORIA *m.* 1840, H.R.H. PRINCE FRANCIS ALBERT, Prince of Saxe-Coburg and Gotha, *son* of ERNEST I, Reigning Duke of Saxe-Coburg and Gotha.

EDWARD VII *m.* 1863, H.R.H. PRINCESS ALEXANDRA CAROLINE MARY, *d.* of CHRISTIAN IX, King of Denmark.

GEORGE V *m.* 1893, H.S.H. PRINCESS VICTORIA MARY AUGUSTA, *d* of H.H. FRANCIS, Duke of Teck.

KING GEORGE VI *m.* 1923 LADY

QUEEN ELIZABETH II *m.*1947

ELIZABETH II FROM THE KINGS OF SCOTLAND

(THE BRUCE)

m. (second) ELIZABETH DE BURGH, *d.* of RICHARD, Earl of Ulster.

DAVID II *m.* JOHANNA, *d.* of EDWARD II of England. No heirs.

SIR ADAM MURE, of Rowallan.

JEAN *m.* SIR JOHN LYON, of Glamis.

SIR JOHN LYON, of Glamis, *m.* his cousin ELIZABETH, *d.* of SIR PATRICK GRAHAM and his wife EUPHEMIA, granddaughter of Robert II.

PATRICK LYON, 1st Lord Glamis, *m.* ISABEL, *d.* of SIR WALTER OGILVY, of Lintrathey.

JOHN (3rd Lord Glamis) *m.* ELIZABETH, *d.* of JOHN SCRYMGEOUR, of Dudhope.

JOHN (4th Lord Glamis) *m.* 1487, ELIZABETH, d. of ANDREW, 2nd Lord Gray.

JOHN (6th Lord Glamis) *m.* JANET, *d.* of GEORGE, Master of Angus.

JOHN (7th Lord Glamis) *m.* 1543, JANET KEITH, sister of the 4th Earl Marischal.

JOHN (8th Lord Glamis) *m.* 1561, ELIZABETH, *d.* of the 5th Lord Abernethy.

PATRICK (9th Lord Glamis) (cr. Earl of Kinghorne, Lord Lyon and Glamis, 1606) *m.* 1595, ANNE, *d.* of JOHN, Earl of Tullibardine.

JOHN (2nd Earl of Kinghorne) *m.* 1641, LADY ELIZABETH MAULE, *d.* of the 1st Earl of Panmure.

PATRICK (3rd Earl of Strathmore and Kinghorne) *m.* 1662, LADY HELEN MIDDLETON, *d.* of the 1st Earl of Middleton.

JOHN (4th Earl of Strathmore and Kinghorne) *m.* 1691, LADY ELIZABETH STANHOPE, d. of the 2nd Earl of Chesterfield.

THOMAS (8th Earl of Strathmore and Kinghorne by Charter 1677) *m.* 1736, JEAN, *d.* of JAMES NICHOLSON, of West Rainton.

JOHN (9th Earl of Strathmore and Kinghorne) (assumed the additional surname of Bowes) *m.* 1767, MARY ELEANOR, *d.* of GEORGE BOWES, of Streatlam Castle.

THOMAS (11th Earl of Strathmore and Kinghorne) *m.* 1800, MARY ELIZABETH LOUISA RODNEY, *d.* of GEORGE CARPENTIER, of Redbourn, Herts.

THOMAS GEORGE (Lord Glamis) *m.* 1820, CHARLOTTE, *d.* of JOSEPH VALENTINE GRINSTEAD.

CLAUDE (13th Earl of Strathmore and Kinghorne) *m.* 1853, FRANCES DORA, *d.* of OSWALD SMITH, of Blendon Hall, Kent.

CLAUDE GEORGE (14th Earl of Strathmore and Kinghorne) *m.* 1881, CECILIA NINA, *d.* of the REV. CHARLES CAVENDISH-BENTINCK.

ELIZABETH ANGELA MARGUERITE

PRINCE PHILIP OF GREECE AND DENMARK

BIBLIOGRAPHY

ANDERSON, JAMES. *Royal Genealogies*. London: James Bettenham, 1732.

ARISTOTLE. *Athenian Constitution*. Trans. Sir F. Kenyon. London: G. Bell & Sons, 1914.

BAIN, GEORGE. 'Celtic art: the methods of construction.' *Scotland's S.M.T. Magazine* 40:4. 1947.

BARNES, EDDIE (Political Editor): 'The Royals who ran from romancing the Stone', from *Scotland on Sunday*, May 7, 2006.

BAYLEY, H. *The Lost Language of London*. London: Jonathan Cape, 1935.

BENTHAM, SIR WILLIAM. *Etruria Celtica - Etruscan literature and antiquities investigated*. Dublin: Philip Dixon Hardy & Sons, 1842.

BLAKE, G.S. *The Stratigraphy of Palestine and its Building Stones*. Palestine Government Stationery Office, 1935. Available from The Palestine Exploration Fund Organisation.

BOECE, HECTOR. *Scotorum historiae a prima gentis origine (The History and Chronicles of Scotland)*. Trans. John Bellenden. Paris, 1527.

BRADLEY, E.T. & M.C. *The Westminster Abbey Guide*. 34th edition. London: Jarrold & Sons Ltd, 1959.

BUCHANAN, GEORGE. *Rerum Scoticarum Historia (The History of Scotland)*. Trans. Aikman. Glasgow: Blackie, Fullarton & Co., 1827.

CHURCHILL, WINSTON S. *The Second World War Vol. III*. London: Cassell & Co. Ltd., 1950.

- - -.   *Thoughts and Adventures*. London: Odhams, 1947.

CONWELL, E. *Ollamh Fodhla*. Bishop Auckland: Covenant Publishing Company Ltd., 2005.

DA COSTA, ISAAC. *Israel and the Gentiles*. 1850. Trans. M. Kennedy in *Noble Families Among the Sephardic Jews*, ed. B. Brewster. Oxford: Oxford University Press/Humphrey Milford, 1936.

DIBELIUS, PROF. WILHELM. *England*. London: Jonathan Cape, 1930.

DIODORUS SICULUS. *Bibliotheca Historica*. Translated by Oldfather, C.H. Cambridge, MA: Harvard University Press, 1935.

ELTON, LORD GODFREY. Imperial Commonwealth. London: Collins, 1945.

ELTON, OLIVER. trans. *The Nine Books of the Danish History of Saxo Grammaticus*. New York: Norroena Society, 1905.

ENCYCLOPAEDIA BRITANNICA 14th edition. 1946. Vol. 7.

GALILEI, VINCENZIO. *Dialogo della musica antica e moderna... in sua difesa contro Ioseffo Zerlino*. Florence: Filippo Giunti, 1581.

GEOFFREY OF MONMOUTH. *The Historia Regum Britannia.* Trans. R. E. Jones, London: Longman, 1929.

GILDAS *Liber querulous de exidio Britanniae (On the Ruin of Britain).* Trans. J.A. Giles, London: Henry G. Bohn, 1848.

GORDON, E.O. *Prehistoric London.* London: Covenant Publishing Company Ltd, 3rd edition, 1932.

GÜNTHER, H. *Racial Elements of European History.* Trans. Wheeler. London: Methuen & Co., 1927

HAMMERTON J. A. ed. *The Harmsworth Encyclopaedia ('Everybody's book of reference').* London: The Amalgamated Press Ltd., 1922-3.

INNES, THOMAS. *A Critical Essay on the Ancient Inhabitants of the Northern Parts of Britain, or Scotland.* London: William Innes, 1729.

JOHANNES DE FORDUN. *Scotichronicon.* Ed. Walter Goodall. Edinburgh, 1759.

JOHN, 3RD MARQUESS OF BUTE. *Scottish Coronations.* Paisley and London,1902.

JOSEPHUS, FLAVIUS *Antiquities of the Jews.* Trans. W. Whiston. Edinburgh: Thomas Nelson, 1843.

KEATING, GEOFFREY. *Foras Feasa ar Éirinn: The History of Ireland.* Eds. D. Comyn, and P.S. Dineen. London: Irish Texts Society, 1902-14.

King George's Jubilee Trust *Official Souvenir Programme of the Coronation of Their Majesties King George VI and Queen Elizabeth.* London: Odhams Press Ltd., 1937.

KNIGHT, CHARLES. *Pictorial History of England.* London: SDUK, 1837.

LATHAM, R.G. *Ethnology of Europe.* London: John Van Voorst, 1852.

LE CARON, MAJOR HENRI. *Twenty Five Years in the Secret Service. The Recollections of a Spy.* London: William Heinemann Ltd., 1892.

LEWIS, SAMUEL ed. *A Topographical History of England.* 1848. [online] Available at http://www.british-history.ac.uk/report.aspx?compid=51078. [Accessed June 2008.]

LOCKYER, SIR NORMAN. *Stonehenge and Other British Stone Monuments Astronomically Considered.* London: Macmillan, 1909.

MACLEOD, FIONA (William Sharp). *Iona.* London: William Heineman, 1912.

MCNEILL, F. MARIAN ed. *An Iona Anthology.* Iona Community, 1990.

MILNER, W. M. H. *The Royal House of Britain an Enduring Dynasty.* London: Covenant Publishing Company Ltd., 1940.

MÜLLER, C. & F. *Fragmenta Historicorum Graecorum*. Paris, 1841-7.

MURRAY, CANON ROBERT HENRY. *The King's Crowning*. London: John Murray, 1937.

NENNIUS *Historia Brittonum (History of the Britons)*. Trans. J.A. Giles, London: George Bell and Sons, 1891.

O'CONOR, CHARLES ed. *Rerum Hibernicarum scriptores veteres iii: Quatuor Magistrorum Annales Hibernici usque ad annum M.CLXXII. ex ipso O'Clerii autographo in Bibliotheca Stowense servato, nunc primum uersione donati ac notis illustrate.(The Annals of the Four Masters)*. London: Buckingham, 1826.

O'DONOVAN, JOHN ed. and trans. *Annála Ríoghachta Eireann (The Annals of the Four Masters)*. Dublin, 1856.

O'DUGAN, JOHN [Seán Óg Ó Dubhagáin]: *The Kings of the Race of Eibhear*. 1635. Trans. M. Kearney. Dublin: John O'Daly, 1847.

Ottawa Correspondent 'Coronation Stone's War-Time Hiding Place'. *The Times* [online] April 9th. 1946: Available at http://archive.timesonline.co.uk/tol/keywordsearch.arc. [Accessed July 2008.]

PALMER, MAJOR H.S. *Ancient History from the Monuments: Sinai*. London: Christian Knowledge Society, 1878.

PAULI, REINHOLD. *König Ælfred und seine Stelle in der Geschichte Englands (The Life of King Alfred)*. Eds. Pauli and T. Wright. London, 1852.

SAYCE, A.H. *The Hittites: The Story of a Forgotten Empire*. London: Religious Tract Society, 1925.

SCHLIEMANN, HEINRICH. *Ilios: The City and Country of the Trojans*. London: John Murray, 1880.

THE SCOTSMAN, 30th December, 1950.

SHEPPARD, STEVE. ed. *The Selected Writings of Sir Edward Coke in 3 Volumes*. Indianapolis: Liberty Fund, 2003.

SKENE, W. F. ed. *Chronicles of the Picts, Chronicles of the Scots and other Early Memorials of Scottish History*. Edinburgh: H M General Register House, 1867.

- - -. 'The Coronation Stone'. *Proceedings of the Society*, Archaeological Data Society Journal, March 8, 1869.

SPELMAN, SIR HENRY. *Concilia, Decreta, Leges, Constitutiones, in re Ecclesiarum Orbis Britannici.* London: R. Badger /P. Stephani & C. Meredith, 1639-64.

SPENCE, LEWIS. *Legendary London: Early London in Tradition and History*. London: R. Hale & Co., 1937.

- - -. *Magic Arts in Celtic Britain.* London: Rider & Co., 1945

STACPOOLE, W.H. *Coronation Regalia: An Excursion into a Curious Bypath of Literature.* London: Whitaker's Almanack Office, 1911.

STANLEY, A.P. *Historical Memorials of Westminster Abbey.* London: John Murray, 1868.

- - -. *Sinai and Palestine.* London: John Murray, 1858.

STEVENSON, J. ed. *Chronicon de Lanercost 1201-1346 (Chronicle of Lanercost).* Edinburgh: Bannatyne Club, 1839.

STOKES, GEORGE. *Lives of the British Reformers, from Wickliff to Fox.* London: Religious Tract Society, 1832.

STUKELEY, WILLIAM. *Abury: A Temple of the British Druids.* London, 1743.

WADDELL, L.A. *The Phoenician Origin of Britons, Scots and Anglo Saxons.* London: Williams & Norgate, 1925.

WAITE, A.E. *The Encyclopaedia of Freemasonry.* London: W. Rider & Son, 1921.

FURTHER READING

Ollamh Fodhla
by E. A. Conwell

The Royal House of Britain
by W. M. H. Milner

Royal Peculiar

History and Destiny of Britain's Royal Throne
by Research Team

Our National Liturgy – The Book of Common Prayer
by A. W. Faith

All books from Covenant Publishing